## BY PATRICIA BEATTY

*Published by*
*William Morrow and Company*

The Bad Bell of San Salvador
Billy Bedamned, Long Gone By
Blue Stars Watching
Bonanza Girl
By Crumbs, It's Mine!
Hail Columbia
How Many Miles to Sundown
I Want My Sunday, Stranger!
Just Some Weeds from the Wilderness
A Long Way to Whiskey Creek
Me, California Perkins
The Nickel-Plated Beauty
O the Red Rose Tree
The Queen's Own Grove
Red Rock over the River
Rufus, Red Rufus
The Sea Pair
Something to Shout About
Squaw Dog
Wait for Me, Watch for Me, Eula Bee

*Published by*
*The Caxton Printers, Ltd.*

Indian Canoe-maker

*Published by*
*McGraw-Hill Company*

The Lady from Black Hawk

❧ *Patricia Beatty*

# Lacy
# Makes
# a Match

William Morrow and Company / New York / 1979

Library of Congress Cataloging in Publication Data

Beatty, Patricia.
　Lacy makes a match.

　Summary: A 13-year-old living in a turn-of-the-century California mining town determines to marry off her adoptive brothers and discover the identity of her real parents.
　[1. California—Fiction.　2. Western stories]　I. Title.
PZ7.B380544Lac　[Fic]　79-9813
ISBN 0-688-22183-1
ISBN 0-688-32183-6 lib. bdg.

Printed in the United States of America.

1　2　3　4　5　6　7　8　9　10

*For Laura Beatty Stewart*

# Contents

# Lacy Makes a Match

# 🖎 1

# A Mighty Welcome Birthday Present!

When you've been left in a basket on someone's veranda and don't know who you are, you have something to think about, all right. For one thing, you feel grateful toward the folks who kept you and raised you, but you feel curious too about who you are and what day your birthday is.

Being left on a veranda is what happened to me, Lacy Bingham, back in the year 1880. Now that it's 1893, and I'm thirteen years old, you can bet your boots that I've done a heap of thinking about myself and who I might truly be.

I haven't come up with any good answers, though. Neither have the Binghams who found me real early on the morning of that April day, howling my head off in the reed basket. They've told me over and over again how Pa Bingham went out with Hector, who was nineteen at the time, to see to the relay horses kept in the corrals. The Binghams had to have horses ready for the next stagecoach coming through Coyote Mountain, the California mining town where they lived. The three boys and Pa would hitch fresh teams to the coaches going in either direction, west and down to San Francisco, or east and over to Denver.

Once Pa spotted me in my basket, he shouted for Ma to come see what showed up in the night. She came out of the stagecoach station in a rush, wearing her nightgown. The other two sons, Michael and Elbert, only a couple of years younger than Hector, followed behind.

How amazed they all were to find a baby girl in an Indian basket, lined with rabbit skins. Although I was wrapped up in a ragged old Indian blanket, I wasn't an Indian. I was a yellow-haired, blue-eyed baby, dressed in a little white nainsook gown with tatting at the hem, and I had a pretty bonnet of white lace with white satin ribbons on my head. That's where I got my name, Lacy.

The Binghams waited and waited for somebody to show up and claim me. All the time, they wondered why their two big dogs never once barked during the night I showed up. They were real barkers, too, watchdogs, not house pets.

But nobody ever did claim me, so after a while the

Binghams took me in as one of their own family. Ma
Bingham had always wanted a girl, anyhow. She gave
me my name and gave me the birthday of April 10, the
day I was left on the veranda. So that's when we always celebrated it, but I knew and they knew it
couldn't truly be my birthday, because I'd been a
couple months old when they found me. I had to be
a winter baby, not a spring one.

The Binghams never tried to make me think I was
a real Bingham. They could have told me that I was,
but that wouldn't have been honest. What's more,
there were folks in Coyote Mountain who knew about
me from the beginning. Ma Bingham didn't want one
of them telling me someday that I wasn't truly a
Bingham and hurting my feelings. If I knew I wasn't
one from the start, I would be used to the idea.

But there was another reason for their not insisting
that I was a real Bingham by blood. You see, I didn't
resemble the rest of them one bit. Pa, who was Jonah
Bingham, and his three sons looked quite a bit alike:
big-boned, brown-headed, and square-jawed. Ma
Bingham had been a tiny lady with black hair, freckles,
and green eyes—nothing like me either.

She was dead and gone now, dead since last Christmas, and, oh, how I missed her! She'd been the only
ma I'd ever known. A baby left on a veranda couldn't
have asked for a better mother or a better pa either.
There was only one fault to be found with the pair
of them. They spoiled folks.

Pa Bingham was very easygoing, and Ma had done

just about everything but breathe for her family. It was my unsaid opinion that her heart truly gave out from overwork, just the way the doctor had said. She'd spoiled the boys, Hector, Michael, and Elbert, something awful. Nothing was too good for them and Pa, or for me. She worked dawn to dusk and far into the night without a word of complaint to give us a comfortable home.

And we were all home, too. Even though the boys were around thirty years old, they were all still living in the big house Pa had built on the slope of Coyote Mountain. When the stagecoach stopped going through, Pa had gone into the livery-stable business, renting out horses and buggies. He was doing real well, and Hector, Michael, and Elbert, who worked for him, were doing real well, too.

But what got my nanny was that they were doing it *at home*! I was housekeeper for the boys now, and I wasn't taking to the chore. Running a big house was full-time work for a full-grown lady. In my time off from school I tried hard as I could to do things the way Ma had, but I wasn't the housekeeper she was.

How those men complained! Pa complained I overstarched his collars. Hector complained I scorched his shirtfront ruffles when I ironed. Michael complained about the way I made his bed. Even Elbert had something to complain about—the lumpy way I darned socks. And they all complained about the food. I couldn't boil water right, according to Michael. My roast meat was either charred or raw and my gravy like brown mud. In the morning everybody wanted his eggs a different way: Pa, poached, Elbert, hard-boiled, so he could stuff them into his overall pockets and eat them later; Hector, fried; and Michael, soft-boiled. Just getting their breakfast wore me out for the rest of the day.

The kind of cooking I did best no one took to day in and day out—beans and bacon, hotcakes, and beef-steaks, camping-out victuals. I soon found out that Pa and the boys, though they doted on camping out in the forest, didn't want to camp out at the supper and breakfast table.

I wasn't any cook and I wasn't any laundress and I wasn't much of a floor scrubber or rug beater either. Instead, I was an eighth-grade girl who didn't know who she truly was, and who right at the moment was wishing she wasn't even a Bingham, so she wouldn't be stuck with the job she'd inherited.

Of course, I soon took up the problem with Pa, who said, "Well, Lacy, honey, Ma ran the house without ever a word that she didn't like what she was doing. But you're right about one thing, she wasn't tryin' to go to school at the same time. Why don't we get some help?"

"Have you got somebody in mind?" I asked.

He sat back in his chair, looking at me over the top of the *Coyote Mountain Daily*, which came out on Tuesday, Thursday, and Saturday with "all the news of the State of California and points East, South, and North." "Lacy, ain't there some ladies in the church who'd help us?"

"No, Pa, there aren't any. They're mostly all married and have houses and families of their own, or they're too old to work the way Ma did."

"Ain't there any widow ladies who don't have families?"

I shook my head. "There are three widow women, Pa. Two of 'em are real old, and the other one, who's a miner's widow, has six kids. She wouldn't come here. We haven't got room for seven more people even if the house is big." I felt close to bawling. "Pa, I need looking after just as much as you and the boys do."

He fingered his starched collar, which was rubbing his neck a bit raw. "Yes, I guess you do."

"Oh, Pa, there aren't any ladies here at all who'll do. Coyote Mountain doesn't attract them. They only come here to live when their menfolks bring 'em here. I hear tell from the butcher that men say there aren't nearly enough single ladies to court."

Pa nodded. "I guess that's so. I reckon ladies think it's too wild, and they don't take to streets shakin' when the miners blast under the town. Well, if there's a shortage of ladies, I guess maybe we'll have to try and get a man to help out."

"A *man*?"

"Yep, a Chinese man. There's five or six of 'em here in town. I'll go see if I can't hire one for us. I hear tell there's lots of folks who have Chinese men workin' for 'em in their houses down in Frisco."

I said, "When you go, Pa, let me go with you."

"Sure, suit yourself, Lacy. Pick out the man you like best."

So after school the next day Pa and I went out to try to hire a Chinese housekeeper.

We might as well have stayed home for all the good it did us. To begin with, there were only four Chinese men, not five or six. Two of them ran a hand laundry. The taller one spoke English well enough to tell Pa that he'd do laundry for us Binghams, but he wouldn't come up to our place to keep house and neither would his little brother. Afterward we went to a small house on Bingham Street, the one named for Pa, rapped on the door, and asked the old pigtailed Chinese man who answered if he wanted to work for us in our house.

He grinned, shook his head, and went outside to show us his garden patch. It was a big one, so we knew he was raising vegetables to sell.

Next we went to a little house just across the street. The Chinese who answered the door was younger and looked plenty powerful. He spoke English, too.

Pa said to him as he had to the others, "Me, Jonah Bingham. Me want you to come cook and clean in my house for me. Come chop-chop, fast. Me pay you good wages."

The Chinese man replied, "Absolutely not!"

"*What?*" Pa looked astonished.

19

The Chinese smiled and went on. "Me got very good job cooking at the Antlers Hotel. Me likee job I got." He quit smiling. "I don't want to be a houseboy to anyone anymore. I did that once before I went to school, and, frankly, me no likee!" And he shut his door.

Pa and I walked away together, red-faced. When we turned onto Main Street, he said, "Well, Lacy, at least we solved the problem of the washing and ironing."

"Yes, Pa, but we still need a cook and cleaner."

He asked, "Can't your friend help you out till school's over, Lacy? That girl with brown hair, buck teeth, and freckles. The one that's homely as sin."

That annoyed me a bit. "Oh, you mean Maud Rowbottom, Pa? She may be homely on the outside, but she's beauteous on the inside, and she's smart as new paint. I'll ask her, but I dunno. She sort of keeps house for her ma already, you know."

"Well, maybe her ma will do it for us!"

I stopped in my tracks to say, "Pa, Mrs. Rowbottom's the town's postmistress!"

I knew that she was danged proud of that job. She had a right to be. Most towns had postmasters, but not Coyote Mountain, California. When Mr. Rowbottom, the postmaster, died, Mrs. Rowbottom had been appointed to his job. She never got married again, though she'd had offers, according to Maud. Her ma didn't want to give up her job as postmistress. Maud said her ma was "wedded to the U.S. Government and the U.S. Mails."

"Yes, that's right, ain't it? I keep forgettin'. It don't

seem natural somehow to have a female postmaster," Pa remarked.

Then I felt even more annoyed. "Pa, I'm sure Mrs. Rowbottom is glad that President Grover Cleveland doesn't feel the way you do about ladies working for the Government! All right, I'll ask Maud to help me out tomorrow. I'll ask her to come other Saturdays, too, if she's willing and her ma will let her."

Maud was willing. That was the one word that really fit her, *willing*, which was why she was my best friend. But even if she was willing, she wasn't eager, although Pa was paying her twenty-five cents for each Saturday. She helped me clean up the kitchen and hang up Ma's handmade parlor afghans and antimacassars on the lines behind the house.

While we were pinning up the last antimacassar Maud said, "Oh, Lacy, I keep forgetting. Ma gave me a letter to give to your folks. It's in the pocket of my apron. It came in on the train from Denver this morning, and it's been done on a typewriting machine."

I answered with my mouth full of clothespins, "Oh, I guess it's another one from O.K. Whipple, the outfit that makes horse harnesses and buggy whips. Pa buys from them now and then. Sometimes O.K. Whipple's letters come here."

I watched her take the letter out of her pocket and look at the envelope. She nodded. "That's right. It's O.K. Whipple, and it isn't addressed to the livery stable. It's for your brother, Hector, not your pa."

21

"Hector does a lot of our ordering for the livery stable. He's probably buying some new black-and-silver harness for the hearse he bought down in Frisco last year. When he went to Denver in February, he got some black ostrich-feather plumes for it."

Maud wasn't much interested in hearing about the hearse. As she stuffed the letter into the pocket of my pinafore, she asked, "Lacy, would you show me your bonnet and baby dress again today?"

"Sure, if you want to see 'em, but you must have looked at 'em ten times already, Maud."

"I know, but the bonnet's so pretty. You must have been a princess, at least, to have a baby hat like that."

I sighed as I turned away from the clotheslines with the basket in my hands, looking down on the town of Coyote Mountain. "Maud, if I'm a princess I've got a queer kind of kingdom. There isn't a castle in sight."

That was true. Gold had been discovered in Coyote Mountain back in 1882, and then silver. The big silver find was played out, but there was still some in the mountain and in the mines that were being worked in tunnels under the town. Coyote Mountain had about six thousand people now, only half as many as in 1885, but they were enough to keep a railroad line going through and a telegraph office.

Pa Bingham had the only livery stable, but there were lots of other businesses. Two banks, a butcher shop, a pharmacy, three other stores including the Emporium, a furniture-and-dry-goods store, a fire station, an opera house, two churches, two doctors, five lawyers, a sheriff, one undertaker and one dentist, an ice-cream parlor, and twelve saloons. Only the opera house and the banks were made out of brick. Everything else was wood.

My whole life had been spent in Coyote Mountain. I hadn't been to Denver or to San Francisco. I knew every inch of my town and most of the families in it. That was why I could say there weren't any ladies free to work for us Binghams.

Maud took up what I'd said about a castle. "No, there aren't any castles, Lacy. There aren't any stone buildings here at all."

"Maud," I said, "I don't think I'm a princess anymore, though I used to when I was little. That was because my baby duds were so fancy, the fanciest anybody had ever seen. Oh, but I'd like to find out who I truly, truly am, Maud! I wish there were some other real, real oldtimers around here besides Pa. I wish Coyote Mountain had had a newspaper when I was left on the veranda. When the editor of the *Coyote Mountain Daily* printed a story asking if anyone knew who I might be, not a soul came forward. All that happened was that a lot of old ladies squinted hard at me in church and now and then squeezed me on the shoulder."

"I know, Lacy, I've seen them." And Maud squeezed me too, to comfort me .

We went up to my room, where I pulled the box I kept treasures in out from under my bed. I pushed aside old school reports and Ma's blue-and-green paisley shawl and brought out the paper in which I kept my baby duds to keep them from yellowing.

"Oh, they're so beautiful," Maud crooned, as she picked up the bonnet and held it to the light. "It's all lace—top, sides, and brim—and the ribbons are pure silk. The lace is just full of roses and scallops and, I guess, three-leaf clovers."

"They sure do look like clovers, don't they? That's what Ma said they were, too. She said the trim on the bottom of the gown is in a pattern she never saw before, a whole lot of little tiny circles on top of each other."

Maud said, "It isn't one bit like the lace in the cap."

"I know. I've been noticing that for years and years." I took the gown back from her, put it and the bonnet into the box, and shoved the box under the bed again. "Come on, Maud, we've got to pick up the dirty duds in Pa's room and in my brothers' to get 'em all ready for the laundryman's mule wagon Monday morning. Getting that done will help me some, but it's only a drop in the work bucket. Speaking of dropping, things are going to change around here or I'm going to drop in my tracks."

"Lead the way, Lacy. Which room do we go to first?"

"Hector's. I'll leave the O.K. Whipple letter on his bed after we've cleaned up his room. Ma called it 'the stable,' but it isn't the worst of the lot by a long shot."

Once I'd opened Hector's window to let the cigar smoke out, I picked up his dirty duds—two ruffle-front

shirts, six pairs of socks, two suits of unmentionables—
all of them tossed on the seat of a chair. After we'd
straightened out his bed, I dumped the letter onto his
pillow. Maud swept his floor and carried the laundry
basket into Pa's room. His weekly shirt and two pairs
of dirty overalls were at the end of his big bed. Even if
he owned the livery stable, Pa didn't put on any fancy
airs. He liked to work with the horses as he always had
while Hector hired out the horses and rigs to front-
office customers.

When we were out in the hall again, Maud asked,
"Lacy, what happened to the basket you showed up
in?"

"Ma used it for our laundry until it fell apart. Then
she bought this one at the Emporium."

"Well, what about the Indian blanket that was
around you? Didn't you tell me you came in an Indian
basket and an Indian blanket?"

"Uh-huh, that's what the Binghams say. Ma said the
blanket was so dirty and torn that she burned it. It
wasn't the kind of special blanket some Indians make.
It was one that white traders sell to Indians. It could
have come from anywhere. The basket was a plain
one without any decorations on it, but Pa thought it
was Indian because of the way it was woven. Come on,
Maud, let's get to Michael's room and Elbert's after
that."

We had some trouble getting Michael's door open
because of all the books behind it. His fiddle and bow

were on his table, and there were more books stacked around them. There were books on the unmade bed, too.

"Where are his dirty things?" asked Maud, as she picked up books while I opened his window.

"Oh, you have to hunt for 'em in his wardrobe over there. He throws them in the bottom so he won't have to look at 'em. He's neater than the other two. He's a bookkeeper, you know." I went to his wardrobe and took out his dirty clothes.

"Does he fiddle better nowadays?" Maud asked me.

"No, Pa says he sounds like two bobcats in a gunnysack. He's grateful he plays a fiddle, not a trumpet."

Maud giggled, and just then the house shook and seemed to slide an inch or so downhill. "Lacy," she said, "they're blasting with dynamite in that old tunnel under your front yard again."

"I guess so, Maud. I wish they'd dig another tunnel in another direction and work in it the rest of the year. Let's get on to Elbert's room and get it over with. It's just across the hall."

We had trouble getting in there, too, because of all the machinery. We had to squeeze past a perpetual-motion machine that didn't work, a miniature steam engine, and something else full of wheels and cogs. The bed was piled high in a tangle of sheets and blankets and dirty duds.

After I'd opened his window to let out the smell of grease, Maud and I sorted out the dirty things from the bedding. First we found two shirts stained with oil

26

from the town's new fire engine. Elbert spent more time tinkering down in the fire station than he did in the stable working for Pa.

"Is this all—two shirts?" Maud asked me.

"No, you never know what you're going to find in here. Come on, Maud." I got down on my hands and knees and reached under Elbert's bed with the broomstick to shove out his other things: a suit of unmentionables, two red neckerchiefs, a pair of oil-stained overalls, and five socks.

"Five!" exclaimed Maud. "And none of them matches any of the others."

"No, of course not. Elbert wears boots. Nobody ever sees his socks. Why should they match?"

She stared at me and then at the five socks with a queer look on her face. Then she said, "But I thought Elbert was handsome and romantic looking! I liked the way his hair flops down. He's the only man his age in town who doesn't have a mustache, too."

"That's because he's too lazy and has his mind too much on machines to take time to shave around a mustache. It's easier to shave straight across his upper lip."

"Don't you like him, Lacy?"

As I picked up the laundry basket, I told her, "Sure, I do. I like all of them, but they're awful hard to live with. I wish all of 'em but Pa would move down to the Antlers Hotel. But they promised Ma on her deathbed that they'd stick around to keep Pa company and would never go off to a hotel."

We went back downstairs together to tie up the laundry bundles and put them on the back porch. Worn out, we sat down with glasses of cold buttermilk from the pantry. As we were talking about school and our teacher and about my birthday, which was tomorrow, and about the cash Pa had promised me as a present, we heard the front door open and slam shut.

Maud stopped telling me how much money she had for the tandem bicycle we wanted to buy and asked, "Who'd that be, Lacy?"

"Hector. That's how he comes in. He moves fast. He's probably home to change his cravat stickpin. He'll find his letter, and then he'll leave in a minute and slam the door again. You can generally tell what Hector's up to. He's noisy by nature."

But I was wrong.

A minute later he pounded down the stairs and through the two parlors and dining room. Then Hector shoved his bowler-hatted head around the edge of the kitchen door and lifted the hat to Maud. "Howdy." He turned to me. "Lacy, I'm packing a valise and carpetbag. I'll be taking the eastbound train to Denver. Tell Pa and the others for me."

"Sure, Hector. Has it got something to do with the letter I put on your pillow?"

His big brown mustache lifted in a grin. "You bet! O.K. Whipple wrote me, 'Sure, come on up to Denver. The deal's on.' Ophelia Katherine Whipple says she's willing to become Mrs. Hector Bingham."

28

## A Mighty Welcome Birthday Present!

I set my glass down hard on the table. "*Ophelia Katherine* Whipple?"

"You bet. Ophelia's got the same initials as her pa, Orville Kenneth. She's his typewriter-machine office worker. She and me will get hitched in Denver and be back here sometime next week to set up housekeeping in the house I rented on El Dorado Street. What do you think about getting a sister-in-law for your birthday present, Lacy?"

"But nobody knows about you getting married or even courting anybody, Hector!" I cried.

"Of course, nobody did. I never told anybody. That way nobody could pester me with jokes about gettin' hitched. So long, Lacy, you tell the town for me!" And he was gone, running upstairs again.

I sat thunderstruck. He could have told me, his only sister, what he was up to. Married? Leaving?

Then all at once I grabbed Maud's hands over the table. "Hector's going to be leaving home for good! That's one less man to pick up after, Maud. It's a queer birthday present, but a mighty welcome one, I guess. He isn't going off to a hotel. He's going to his own house with a wife in it."

When she got very excited, Maud's yellowish eyes glowed like a cat's. "Oh, Lacy, that's the ticket. Get the other two married, too. If Hector can do it, they can too, can't they? That way your ma would be happy up in Heaven and so would everyone else—especially you."

"Uh-huh," I breathed. "Especially me."

## ✥ 2

# One Down, Two to Go

I didn't help Hector pack his duds or see him off at the train depot either. And I didn't go down to the livery stable to tell Pa and Michael and Elbert what Hector was up to. One of them might try to stop him before he got on the train, thinking he was being hasty. I figured I'd tell them all at the supper table that there was an Ophelia Katherine Whipple as well as an Orville Kenneth. That ought to take their minds off the food—fried ham, fried potatoes, fried eggs, and fried leftover apple pie from the night before. Maud and I had decided frying it might soften up the crust.

So she and I houseworked together the rest of that Saturday, and while we did we talked some about

Hector's running off to get married, but mostly we talked about Michael and Elbert.

"I never heard of a bridegroom eloping, did you?" she asked. "I thought only brides did that."

"Of course not. If one of 'em elopes, the other one has to, too." I began to fold the linen table napkins she was ironing. "Now that I've had time to get over the surprise, I've decided that what Hector's up to is very romantic. And he was smart to keep it a secret all along. Nobody suspected for a minute what was in those letters he kept getting from O.K. Whipple. Now that I think about it, he got plenty of 'em, too. If Pa or Elbert had found out, they'd have joshed Hector day and night. There aren't any flies on Hector all right. He sure is smart. He stole a march on 'em, and I'm glad for him."

As Maud clanged the flatiron down into the holder on the stove top, she said, "Uh-huh, and you're glad, too, that he's one less mouth to cook for."

"You bet. One less mouth means less dishes and less picking up after."

While we struggled to get the ironing board into its closet, she said, "Lacy, does it appear to you that Michael and Elbert might elope, too?"

"I dunno, Maud. Michael's a deep one. He might be getting secret letters at the livery stable, because he opens the mail there. Elbert's not so deep, but you can never tell about him either. He could be getting mail from some lady at the fire station and not letting us know. Hector was smart to have his Ophelia Whip-

31

ple letters come to the house, or Michael could have opened one of them and found out what was up. I don't know."

"Well, I do know, Lacy." My best friend lowered her voice. "I sort the mail for my ma lots and lots of times. Your other two brothers never get letters written to them at all. Only your pa does in the name of the livery stable, and sometimes Hector. Naturally, with you being so friendly to me, every time I spot the name Bingham on a letter, I take notice of it. Now, Lacy, don't stare at me like that. I'm interested in your family, not nosy."

I patted her arm. "I was just thinking, that's all. No sir, it doesn't appear to me that Michael or Elbert has any intention of getting married, let alone eloping."

"Maybe Hector will give them the idea," she said. "For your sake, we can hope so. But if not, Lacy, you ought to take a hand in matters."

"What should I do?"

"Try to get your other brothers to find themselves wives, too. Then they'll be sure to move out fast. Ma says that two women don't live happily together under one roof unless they're ma and daughter. She says all brides want homes of their own right away and want to make their husbands happy in them. She says brides will put up with a lot of catering to a man that even mothers and sisters won't do. She says that's another reason why she won't get married again. She's already been a bride and remembers it well."

I nodded. Mrs. Rowbottom was a very respected lady in Coyote Mountain and was considered mighty smart, even if Pa didn't cotton to her being postmistress.

All at once Maud asked, "Lacy, who's the prettiest girl in town?"

I stopped pushing up and down on the kitchen pump to get water for the teakettle and, being loyal to her, said, "I guess maybe you are, Maud Rowbottom."

"No, I don't mean you or me, Lacy." She was giggling. "I mean somebody the right age for Michael or Elbert."

The answer was easy. "Belle Cantrell down at the Emporium, the dentist's daughter. She's the right age and getting older—she's almost thirty, I guess—and she's pretty as a picture, too. The only other unmarried ladies in town are the dance-hall girls."

Maud's face grew long and solemn. "The dance-hall girls wouldn't do. They paint their cheeks with something out of a jar called rouge. Lacy, I think you ought to start talking a lot about Belle and how nice and good and pretty she is and how she's getting old and how your brothers aren't getting any younger either. How old are they, anyhow?"

"Hector's thirty-two, Michael's thirty, and Elbert's almost twenty-nine."

Maud gave me her wisest look. "That's getting up there, you know."

"I guess it is." I looked at my hands. They were

work worn and red, and my fingernails were broken and ragged, the way Ma's little hands used to be. "In a way it would be a kindness to Michael and Elbert, if I tried to get them happily married wouldn't it? After all, I owe a lot to the Bingham family for taking me in when I was a baby."

"You surely do, Lacy. Here's your chance to pay them back. Your ma wouldn't mind if they left home to be happy in homes of their own with loving little wives." Maud's eyes glowed yellow and smoky. "And I'd be glad to help you whenever you need me."

"Maud Rowbottom, you are the best friend a girl ever had."

"Thank you, Lacy. I could say the same for you. Remember, all you have to do is ask me in case you run into any trouble. I'm not helping you today just because of the twenty-five cents your pa is paying me. I would have worked here for nothing."

"You're a true-blue brick."

"Now remember," said Maud, "even if it's one down with Hector gone, you've still got two to go, and those other two could be tough nuts to crack!"

I told Pa and Michael and Elbert the big news the minute we all sat down to supper.

"Hector won't be here tonight. If you're wondering where he is, he's eloped," I said, as I started to cut up my fried ham.

Michael stopped eating, his fork halfway to his

mouth. Elbert grabbed at his throat because he'd just swallowed. Pa took so much hot coffee in one sip that his face turned red with pain.

"*Eloped?* Hector?" Pa exclaimed a moment later.

"Who did Hector elope with and where did he go?" demanded Michael while Elbert coughed.

"With O.K. Whipple up in Denver," I said.

Pa was angry. "O.K. Whipple's a man with a long, white beard. I know the old galoot. What're you up to, Lacy?"

I poked at my fried egg, which was very leathery around its edges. "Well, I guess you don't know he had a daughter, Ophelia Katherine. She's her pa's typewriter operator. Hector has been secretly writing to her for a while. He asked her to marry him, and she said Yes in the letter he got just today. So he packed up and took the train to Denver, where he's going to marry her."

"My Lord." Michael snorted. "Hector could have told me."

"Keeping it so secret's a low-down thing for him to do," mumbled Elbert.

Pa demanded, "Lacy, how come you know about it and we don't? Did Hector tell you?"

I took a bite of stringy ham and egg, then said, "Nope, he didn't tell me. He didn't tell a single soul hereabouts. Maud Rowbottom and me know because we happened to be here in the house working, and I suppose Hector wanted to tell somebody rather than

35

leave a note about what he was up to. He did say he kept it secret because he didn't want to be joshed."

"Is he coming back?" Pa wanted to know.

"He says he is. He says he's rented a house here and will be back pretty soon."

"What did you say to him when he told you, Lacy?" asked Michael.

"I should have told him I hoped he would be happy, but I didn't. I was too surprised to think of that."

"Good Lord," muttered Pa. "Hector a married man! I never thought he'd get hitched. I thought all he'd do the rest of his life would be hitch horses. Well, I do hope he'll be happy."

After I'd polished off my fried potatoes, I said, "Maud says that her ma says men thrive on being married." I was firing the first shot in my campaign to marry off Michael and Elbert, though they didn't know it yet.

Pa sighed. "Yep, that's true enough. I fared better when Ma was here. No offense to you, Lacy, but marriage is better for man or beast than being solo."

Well, this was something! Pa was on my side! "Mrs. Rowbottom says that an old bachelor is one of nature's most miserable creatures. An old maid can cook and sew for herself, but most old bachelors look like last year's bird's nests."

I took note that both Michael and Elbert had their heads bent over their plates, shoveling in my grub even though they didn't much like what I'd cooked.

The time had come to fire my biggest gun. "Michael, you're the next oldest. Why don't you get married to somebody nice, too?"

He jerked his head up to glare at me. "Maybe I can't find anybody who suits me. Have you got anybody in mind?"

"Yes, I have. Belle Cantrell. Why don't you take her to the opera house or out buggy riding? Maud says that lots of town bachelors are sparking Belle." I hadn't heard that from Maud, but I felt Michael might be more impressed if he thought the information didn't come from me.

He mumbled, "She might tell me No, particularly if she's got the whole town on her string."

"Pooh. Faint heart ne'er won fair lady, Michael Bingham." I stood up to take away the plates. "It's fried apple pie for dessert. That's all we've got. I hear Belle Cantrell is a real good cook when it comes to Lady Baltimore cake and chocolate fudge."

The next day, my birthday, was on Sunday, and Pa and Michael and I went to church as always, while Elbert went to the fire station to polish the Silsby steam-powered fire-engine. It had come to Coyote Mountain from Frisco only two months ago and hadn't been called out to any fires so far, but I suspected the brass trim on it had been shined up so many times by so many volunteer firemen that it was worn down to next to nothing.

Elbert left at Main Street while the rest of us walked on to the church on El Dorado Street. I had on the white muslin dress I wouldn't wear much longer. By September I'd be wearing long skirts and putting my hair up on top of my head, and I'd be going by wagon to high school in Osborne Valley, ten miles to the south. Luckily that was only six months away because the white dress and most of the other things Ma had sewed for me were getting too tight in lots of places.

Pa was dressed in his brown go-to-meeting suit and looked just fine. But, oh, that Michael! He looked exactly like what he was, a bookkeeper, in the black suit and vest that Hector had handed down to him. It had been Hector's go-to-funerals suit, and Michael wore it with a black cravat, black shoes, and a black felt hat that sat straight across his dark eyebrows. To look at him, you'd never guess he tried to play romantic Gypsy tunes on his fiddle. When he took his hat off, matters got worse. He parted his hair straight down the middle and had it cut as short as possible on the sides so it couldn't curl over his ears. His mustache didn't droop softly. It curled a bit and bristled in spite of the wax he used.

I sighed as we walked along, then finally gave him a nudge with the point of my parasol. "Belle Cantrell will be singing in the choir, Michael. Why don't you wave to her up there in the choir loft?"

He said, "Don't be foolish. Besides, how will she know it's her I'm waving at? There are quite a few ladies in the choir."

38

"She's the only one who isn't married. Would you be waving to married ones? Why don't you ask her to go buggy riding after church?"

"I haven't got a buggy, Lacy. We're walking."

"You could get a buggy from the livery stable. You work there. It wouldn't cost you anything, you know."

I heard Pa chuckling on the other side of me.

Michael looked down at me and said, "You sure got Belle Cantrell on the brain, haven't you? What're you trying to do? Get rid of me? Make me marry her when I don't even really know her?"

In my sweetest voice I said, "I think it would be very good for you and for Elbert, too, to get married."

Michael asked with a snort, "Who'd marry Elbert?"

"I don't know, but I'm sure somebody would. Maud's ma says there's a Jill for every Jack. Lots of ladies think Elbert's romantic looking, but they think you look like an old-maid bookkeeper in britches. They think you couldn't get a lady to consider you as a husband."

"Who is *they*?" That last had got him. He stopped in his tracks, and I saw that his jaw muscles had tightened.

"Oh, girls I know at school."

"Like Maud Rowbottom, huh?"

"Well, yes, her, too."

"Lacy!" Pa warned, so I shut up as we reached the steps of the church.

Maud was there along with her ma and her five-year-old brother, Harvey, who was struggling to get loose from his mother's hand. As we passed by, I whispered into Maud's ear, "I told 'em all about Hector's romantic eloping, and I'm working hard as ever I can on Michael."

"Is that why he looks so mad right now?" she whispered back.

I nodded, said good morning to Mrs. Rowbottom, and, dodging a kick Harvey was aiming at my ankle, went inside. Michael was the one who got the kick instead. Naturally, Mrs. Rowbottom smacked Harvey, making him howl, but Michael's temper didn't improve one bit. I could hear him snorting all through the sermon, and he didn't sing at all from the hymnal we shared.

We Binghams went out together afterward, shaking hands at the door with the preacher. Then we milled around and talked to friends and livery-stable customers. Pa went off to jaw with one of the town doctors, but to my surprise Michael stayed with me. I supposed he was about to tell me privately what he thought of the way I was acting, but before he got the chance, Maud came up to me dragging Harvey with her. Michael stalked off with his hands in his pockets without even asking how she was.

I watched him. Was he going home in a huff? No, he was headed the wrong way. I clutched at Maud. "Look, he's going up to the Cantrell carriage!"

So he was. He went right up to Belle, who looked

mighty handsome in pale-yellow silk with a big black straw hat. Before she could get up beside her pa on the seat, Michael tipped his hat to her and started talking. Was he asking her to go buggy riding with him? Maud, Harvey, and I started edging closer, but before we could get there, the talk between Michael and Miss Cantrell was over. I saw Belle shake her head and point to one of the town's young lawyers, who was leaning up against a pine tree talking to a miner.

"Look at your brother scowl!" Maud whispered to me.

He surely was scowling. He passed Maud and her brother and me as if we were mashed toads in the road. Only after Michael was some steps past us did he call back over his shoulder, "I'm taking her to the operetta next month. It's the first time she's got free. Are you satisfied, Lacy Bingham?"

"Next month!" I exclaimed. That was days and days away.

Maud touched my arm. "Lacy, maybe you can speed up their romance."

I shook my head. "I don't even know that they like each other yet."

Maud gave me a wise nod. "Well, he did ask her, didn't he? If he didn't like her at all, would he have asked her? Would he have done it just to please you?"

"No, he wouldn't. I guess she must like him some, too, or she wouldn't say Yes to anything."

41

"That's true, Lacy. Why don't you go down to the Emporium and find out how she feels about him?" Maud made a grab at Harvey and caught him by his long curls before he could chase after a dog that was running by. Harvey was surely a handful.

"But I hardly know Belle Cantrell," I said. "I haven't said more than hello to her all my life. Ma did all the talking when she bought calico and gingham and lace and things like that."

Lace! Just mentioning the word gave me a thought. It was a good one, too, one I should have had a long time ago.

"All right, Maud, I'll go see Belle. I'll go tomorrow right after school."

My, but Miss Cantrell was pretty close up! She had white skin, big chocolate-colored eyes, and hair that was a cross between yellow and red. She smelled of lavender eau de cologne and was elegant, too, even in her high-collared black-silk clerk's dress with a yellow tape measure hanging around her neck.

Miss Cantrell knew me right off. In a low voice she asked, "What can I do for you, Lacy? Do you need some cloth?" She laughed. "This seems to be my week for Binghams."

I said, "I brought something to show you. Something I want to ask you about." I laid my baby cap and the little gown on the counter in front of her. "These are what I was wearing when I got left on the Bingham stagecoach-station veranda thirteen years ago yesterday. I suppose maybe you heard about how I came to live with the Binghams."

"Oh, yes, just about everybody who isn't a newcomer knows about that. So you were wearing these clothes?"

"Yes, ma'am, even if I was in an Indian basket. Did Ma Bingham ever bring these duds to you?"

"No, she never did." While Miss Cantrell held the lace bonnet to the light, she said softly, "I want to tell you how sorry I am about her death. She was one of my very favorite customers. You know, this is very unusual lace in the cap."

I mumbled more to myself than to her, "I wonder why Ma never fetched it to you, what with you selling lace and stuff like that."

Belle Cantrell looked at me understandingly. "I suspect she didn't want to open up the question of who you truly were after she'd raised and got so attached to you. She didn't ever talk to folks about how you came to her, you know. Somebody else told me your story, not your mother."

"Maybe so," I said. "Do you know anything about the lace or the tatting trim on the gown?"

She was shaking her head as she put down the cap and took up the baby dress. "No, I've never seen lace like it, and this isn't tatting at all. It's crochet lace, hand-done crochet lace, but in a pattern that's unfamiliar to me." She returned the baby duds to me. "But I don't claim to be any real expert on lace. I only sell ladies what's sent up here from San Francisco and

43

Denver." She put her finger to her cheek as I put the things back into a bag and asked, "Can you draw or sketch, Lacy?"

"A little bit, sure."

"All right. There's a shop in San Francisco that sells only laces and trims. I'll give you the name and address. You can draw a picture of the lace and trim patterns and send the sketches with a letter asking what the people at the shop know about them. They are real experts, and they will reply. The cap is very beautiful. I suspect it's handmade lace, and then it would be very expensive."

I watched Miss Cantrell open a drawer under her counter and take out a little white card. She copied an address from it onto a piece of paper and gave it to me. "Gosh, thank you. I'll let you know what they have to say."

"Fine, Lacy, I'd like that. This is exciting. Finding what kind of lace it is could give you some idea of who your real family might be."

"Yes, ma'am." I went on to other business. "My brother Michael says he's taking you to an operetta at the opera house next month."

"That's right, Lacy. It's supposed to be a very funny operetta. I'm looking forward to seeing it." She smiled at me.

That was good. I smiled right back at her. "I know he wishes it was sooner than next month. I bet that's what he was wishing when you told him you were all tied up until that time. I bet you surely have a lot of beaux—just about every gent here and down in Osborne Valley, too."

"Yes, Lacy, I do have a number of beaux, but you know this is the very first time, though I went to school with your brothers here, that any one of the Bingham men has asked me to go anywhere with him."

I felt I should apologize for them, so I said, "They're sort of shy, I guess. But they can give a lady some surprises now and then." I told her about Hector eloping.

She only nodded. "I hope he will be very happy, and I'll look forward to meeting his bride." She picked up a bolt of blue calico and put it back on the shelf behind her. "Haven't your other brothers ever taken anyone buggy riding? There were a number of single girls hereabouts last year."

"No, they never have, not that I can remember."

With her back to me, she said very softly, "Now that's too bad, isn't it? They're rather good-looking, too."

I would have talked more to her about both brothers, but just at that moment a lady came up behind me and asked, "Haven't you got that black soutache braid in yet that I asked for last week, Belle? I need it to trim that cape."

## ⚘ 3

# The Letter from Frisco

Main Street started shaking while I was out on the front porch of the Emporium, thinking about the surprise Belle Cantrell had given me, so I hooked one arm around a porch post to steady myself. Apparently Belle wanted to be courted by my brother Elbert, too. I'd never guessed she'd taken any note of him, but when he got duded up for the Fourth of July parades in his shiny fireman's helmet, scarlet flannel shirt, and striped trousers he did cut a handsome figure. His boots were black rubber and plenty high enough to hide his mismatched socks.

While Main Street went on shaking and rattling, I made up my mind to two things.

46

First of all, I'd tell each of my brothers that Miss Cantrell liked him, without letting the other one know. That ought to give both of them hope. By rights, Belle ought to marry Michael, because he was the oldest, but if she preferred Elbert. . . . Well, it was her choice, not mine. She was the one getting married.

The other thing I decided was to get hold of Maud right away and tell her about the lace shop down in Frisco.

The next day after school Maud and I drew the sketches in black ink on white paper, and I wrote a letter to go along with them. I enclosed a stamped envelope addressed to me so the Frisco folks would reply. Then Maud postmarked it for her ma and put my letter into the canvas mail sack that would go out on the train the next day at twelve o'clock.

I wondered as I walked home from Maud's kitchen how long it would take for the lace experts to send me an answer and what they would say. This was surely exciting, as Belle had said.

And I had something else to wonder about, too. Mrs. Hector. Ophelia Katherine Whipple Bingham. What would she be like? Would she like us? I hoped she'd be a little bit like Ma in her nature, kind and gentle so Pa could find her a comfort. I didn't expect her to come up and do our housework, not when she had a rented place of her own, but maybe she'd ask the rest of us Binghams to supper sometimes. I hoped she would be a good cook and a good seamstress, because I was in need of somebody like that.

I hadn't let out one word of complaint on Sunday, but except for Michael's asking Belle Cantrell out, it had been a pretty sad thirteenth birthday for me. There hadn't been any cake, the way there always was when Ma had been with us. Pa hadn't forgotten me, though. He'd given me fifty cents, and Michael and Elbert had given me two bits each. At least, the cash meant I could put something more toward the bicycle-built-for-two that Maud and I had been looking at for a long time in the Sears and Roebuck catalog.

Hector fetched his bride home at the end of the week, escorting her up our front steps as if she was made out of spun sugar and might break. She was sort of a spun-sugar lady at that—tall and willowy with pale-blond hair, creamy skin, and round, light-blue eyes. Her traveling suit was cream-colored silk, and her big yellow straw hat was covered with peach-colored roses and two turtledoves that stuck their wings out over the sides.

"This here's my little wife," Hector announced the minute she was inside the parlor. "We only came up here now to say hello, and then we'll go back down to the Antlers Hotel and live there until Ophelia gets our little house fit to move into." Hector motioned to her. "All right, all of you. Come on, kiss the bride. You first, Pa, then the rest of you."

Ophelia gave her cheek to Pa, who grinned after

48

he kissed her. Then came Michael and Elbert, blushing to the tops of their ears.

"Lacy, you too," ordered Hector.

I came up to my new sister-in-law, my queer birthday present, curtseyed, and standing on tiptoes laid my freckled cheek against her cool, white one. She smelled of orange-flower talcum powder.

She had a kiss and a hug for me and said, "I hope we'll be the very best of friends, Lacy."

I said, "I hope so, too."

Hector burst out, "I have to tell you the truth, Mike and Elbert. I never been so cussed happy in all my born days as I am right now. I should 'a found my Ophelia years and years ago and hitched up with her that very day. I never knew it, but I was cut out for life in double harness all along. Mike, my boy"—here he went over to Michael and playfully punched him on the shoulder—"get yourself a pretty little bride of your own and be as happy as I am. Elbert, the same goes for you. Stop mooning all the time over machinery and look for a sweet-natured little female woman, who'll make you the light of her life."

I was thrilled to pieces with Hector's speech, the longest I had ever heard him give. He'd told them just the right thing. I couldn't have asked for better.

Pa put in, "We're sure glad to hear it. I think I'm speakin' for all of us when I say that Hector has got himself one of the prettiest ladies I ever set eyes on. You know, you don't look one bit like your old pa."

She had a nice laugh. "No, I take after my mother's

side of the family. But Mr. Bingham, how would you ever know? My father has had his face covered with whiskers ever since the Civil War."

"She's got you there!" exploded Hector, who, I'd decided by now, was acting a bit silly with happiness.

All at once I heard Michael behind me say quietly to Elbert, "Hector's happy as a bear climbing a bee tree. If you want to ask him to lend you some cash, now would be a good time, Elbert."

"Nope," muttered Elbert. "You don't have to rub it in that I'm dead broke from buying machine parts. I'm glad old Hector's happy. Maybe you're sort of jealous that he is."

"No, I'm not. Hector isn't the only one who can get married if he has a mind to," Michael said fiercely.

I enjoyed overhearing this discussion, but, alas, it didn't go on. Hector and his wife were leaving, so everybody had to go out onto the front porch and see them down the steps. Hector helped her down just as he had helped her up.

Once the newlyweds were gone, I said to both of my brothers, "That's the way a lady likes to be treated by a gent. That's the way you ought to treat Miss Cantrell when you take her places, like she'd bust in two if you aren't careful with her."

Elbert looked at me and grumbled, "I ain't taking her any place."

"Don't you think she's pretty, Elbert?" I asked.

"Sure, she's pretty enough, I guess, prettier than some other ladies in town."

He had noticed. Good. "Belle hinted to me that she wouldn't take unkindly to being courted by both of the Bingham men at the same time. After all, the rest of the town bachelors are sparking her." I rushed on because this chance might be the only one I got. "What I say is let the best man win the fair lady, and let him be a Bingham."

Pa added, "The Cantrells are good stock, fine folks. I know you plan to court the gal, Michael, but do you like her, too, Elbert?"

"I haven't got anything against her, Pa. I guess maybe I'll ask her to come and see the new fire engine and watch us drill. After all, I saved her two pug dogs off her balcony during the fire at her house two years ago. I stuffed a dog in the top of each one of my boots when I came down the ladder. She liked that."

Pa turned to Michael. "Is it goin' to cause bad feelings between you and Elbert if you both court her?"

"I don't see why it should, Pa," Michael answered.

My, but things were going well! I could hardly believe what I was hearing. I still had something else to say, but it would come a bit later. I went out to the kitchen to get the lemonade I'd made in case the newlyweds wanted some refreshments. When I returned, Pa and my brothers were talking about what kind of wedding present to give Mr. and Mrs. Hector. Finally they decided on a barrel of good whiskey, which I thought was dreadful.

I waited until everyone had finished his lemonade. Then I went around with the tray to get the empty glasses. As I went by Pa, I leaned down and kissed him on the cheek. Dear Pa, he was as lonesome as I was. How we both missed Ma!

Next I went to Michael, and as I took his glass I whispered, "I do believe that Belle Cantrell likes you better than any man in town." He looked startled; then a smile crossed his face.

I went over to Elbert and bent down to get his glass, saying, "Elbert, I do believe that Miss Cantrell likes you better than any man in town since you saved her pug dogs in the fire."

He didn't look quite as startled as Michael. Elbert turned red as a beet, got up without a word, and went out onto the porch. He stood looking down over Coyote Mountain, and after a while I saw a grin spread over his mouth.

Later that same day I went to the post office to tell Maud about the new couple. Mrs. Rowbottom, a thin, little lady with graying hair, came out into the parlor while I was talking to Maud and stood for a minute listening to me.

"Lacy," she said, "newlyweds are usually happy, but it doesn't always last, you know."

"But Pa and Ma Bingham were always happy," I cried.

"Yes, they were lucky. They had a good marriage. Good ones are made in Heaven."

Suddenly I was hit with an awful thought. "Well, if a marriage turns out bad, does the husband ever move back in with his pa and ma?"

"Almost never, Lacy."

I let out a sigh and clutched my stomach.

Maud told me once her ma had gone, "Don't worry. He won't come back. What about your other two brothers, though?"

As I leaned toward her, my foot hit something under her parlor table. I lifted the velvet cloth to see what it was. Was it a pillow? No, it was Harvey. He gave me a funny look, but he didn't scoot out from underneath.

"What's he doing under there?" I asked Maud.

"Eavesdropping. Spying. It's the latest thing he's taken up," she explained. "Ignore him. Ma says it won't last. He'll give it up when he starts to school. He's awful smart, Lacy, and he's so danged bored these days that he listens in on folks for entertainment. Ma says once he begins to read, he'll be all right again."

I let the velvet cloth fall and went on. "Well, both of my brothers are going to court at the same time a certain lady who works in the Emporium. Why not have both of them in the running? There are a heck of a lot of horses in that race already."

Maud's eyes had started glowing. "I think it's the most romantic thing I ever heard of. Both of them smitten with the same lady. Maybe it will lead to a duel, swords or pistols or that sort of thing."

"Maud Rowbottom, that's a dreadful thing to say! And you upset Harvey, too. He just grabbed me by the ankle."

"Let go, Harvey," she ordered him. "I was only joshing you, Lacy. So you say Hector is happy now."

"Happy as a clam."

"Lacy, I might as well tell you something right now. For years people here in town have said that your ma should have worked at marrying off her boys instead of keeping 'em tied to her apron strings so long. Now you're doing what she should have done, and I'm proud of you."

"Thank you, Maud."

Ten days passed and not a thing happened, except that I got to know Mrs. Hector better and decided more and more that my brother had done himself proud. She didn't invite us to dinner, though, since they were living in the Antlers Hotel. Instead, she gave all her time to fixing up the little house on El Dorado Street.

As for me, I was falling behind. Having the laundry done by the Chinese brothers was a big help, and having Maud with me on Saturdays was fine, too, but I was getting behind not only with the housework but with my schoolwork. Examination time was coming soon, and sometimes I was too worn down with house chores to study the way I wanted to. For the first time ever I was having a hard time memorizing the Longfellow poetry I used to find to easy. What seemed to push the lines out of my brain was the constant list of things we needed at the butcher shop or the grocery store or thinking up what I could cook that somebody would eat without complaining all the way through the meal.

In spite of my weariness, I noticed that my brother Michael seemed worn out too. Or else he was more and more nervous. I supposed it was all that waiting he had to do before the time came to take Belle Cantrell to the operetta. Nothing I did suited him. I couldn't make his bed right. My cooking gave him heartburn. He kept saying he could barely wait to taste Mrs. Hector's cooking, because no matter how bad it might be it had to be better than mine. We were all waiting for that.

I was waiting, too, to hear from the lace shop down in Frisco. To Maud I complained that probably my letter hadn't got there, but she said that never happened with the United States Mails. She felt I would surely get a reply, because I'd sent a stamped envelope and people just couldn't resist using them.

At last, on a Saturday at the very tail end of the month, I got a letter from Frisco.

Maud brought it to me, running up our hill to the front door.

"Is it it?" I shouted to her as I opened the door.

"It's it!" she shouted back at me.

I grabbed it from her hand and said, "Maud, let's go up to my bedroom and read it privately."

We ran upstairs, I shut my door, and we sat on the bed together while I opened the envelope.

The letter was addressed to Mademoiselle Bingham, and it said:

I have looked with care at the pen-and-ink sketches you have sent to this shop. The lace in the infant cap you describe is handmade and most unusual. We do not sell such lace here in San Francisco. It is not made in the United States. I have consulted a book of lace patterns we have, and it is my opinion that this is Carrickmacross lace. That lace is made by appliqueing a pattern by hand onto a net background. The motifs used in Carrickmacross lace are the rose, scallops, and shamrocks, not, as you say, three-leaf clovers.

As for the crochet trim on the bottom of the baby gown, I was not able to identify it for certain because your sketch was not clear enough. Could you please snip off a bit of this trim and send it to me by mail, so I can see and touch the texture of the thread? Then perhaps I can tell you something about it, too, for I suspect I know already what it is.

Yours truly,<br>Madame Thérèse

P.S. Carrickmacross lace is made in only one place in the world, Ireland.

"*Ireland?*" I said the name in a shocked whisper.

"Golly," breathed Maud. "You know for sure that you aren't a true Bingham, but maybe you aren't even a real American. What do Irish people look like, anyhow?"

All I could do was shake my head while I tried to

take in this strange and unexpected information. Finally I told her, "I don't know what they look like. I never met anybody from Ireland. But I'm sure of one thing. Irish babies wouldn't travel around in Indian baskets wrapped up in Indian blankets!"

## ≈ 4

# Michael Goes Courting

Neither Maud nor I knew what to make of the letter from Madame Thérèse, but we had to decide how I was going to answer it.

"I'll snip off a piece of the crochet lace right now." I said. "There's a place where it sort of laps over. Then we'll put it inside an envelope and send it with another stamped one of mine to her. I ought to write her a note thanking her for what she's doing when I'm not buying anything from her, too."

"Sure. You can do it now, and I'll take the letter down and put it in the mailbag for Frisco. Oh, Lacy, this is so exciting! I didn't ever expect to hear that you might be a foreigner."

I didn't truly like what she was saying, but I held my temper because best friends didn't grow on trees. Hearing that I might not be an American was a jolt, but, on second thought, what did the Irish lace on the bonnet prove? After all, I could be an American baby, and somebody could have given me a cap of Irish lace. Maybe a godmother or a grandmother had given it to my true ma for me. She might have bought it as a present in some fancy store somewhere back East. I knew that the lace was expensive, but maybe my true folks had been rich and bought the cap for me because it was pretty, not because it was Irish. Maybe my real folks were still rich! Maybe I'd been kidnapped. Did California Indians go in for kidnapping? I'd never heard that they did, but I wasn't any expert on them either. Maybe. Maybe. Maybe. All the maybe's were enough to make me dizzy.

Once I'd cut off the crochet lace and written a note and got the two envelopes ready, I decided to go down to the post office with Maud. I was too excited to sit still at home, and I didn't have the heart to begin some household chore that I didn't want to do in the first place.

As we passed the barbershop on our way to the post office, Maud pointed to the window and said, "Look, Lacy, your brother Michael's in there in the barber chair. He's getting his hair cut."

I glanced quickly at the window, wishing that Michael had waited. "Yep, that's him all right. He's getting himself scalped. He thinks cutting almost all of his hair away makes him look neat, and he wants to look good for tomorrow night when he takes Miss Cantrell to the operetta."

"Oh dear, he doesn't look one bit romantic." Maud put her arm around my shoulders. "I've got a brother, too, remember? You've got old ones, and I've got a baby one. Men don't think the way we do, you know. Young as he is, I've learned that from Harvey."

"Doesn't he ever talk, Maud? Does he tell you about his spying game?"

"Lordy, does he talk, but only to Ma and me so far. When Harvey opens up someday, he'll jaw the ears off a mule and make the whole town run. He'll be president of this country if nobody shoots him first."

All I felt I could safely say was, "Ummm." Anyway, I had other things on my mind. So I forgot about Harvey and concentrated on the letter from Madame Thérèse. What should I do? Should I tell the Binghams and Miss Cantrell, too?

As I walked back home, I decided not to tell anybody, at least not yet. After all, Madame Thérèse was supposed to write me again about the crochet lace on the baby dress. I'd wait until I had more information from her. Then I'd tell Pa and, after him, Belle Cantrell. I was sure Belle would be interested in what I'd learned today, but I didn't want to go see her until she'd had time to be sparked by my brother Michael and maybe by Elbert, too. I didn't know if Elbert had asked her to a fire drill yet, because every time I brought up her name at the supper table he'd say,

"Please pass the steak sauce, Lacy," and start talking horse gear and engines with Pa and Michael.

Last night I'd broken in to ask, "Elbert, are you taking some lady to the firemen's ball in June?" It was one of the big events of the year in Coyote Mountain. He looked me right in the eye and said, "Sure, don't I always take a lady? Didn't I always take Ma to it? Well, this year I'm going to take you, Lacy. You know just as well as Ma did that I can't dance, so I have to take a lady from the family. She won't fret if I go over in a corner and talk with the other firemen and let her dance all night with anybody who asks her."

Oh, that Elbert! I was irked and would have said something, but before I had the words set in my mind, Michael put in, "Because I'm musical by nature, I can dance the waltz, Varsouvienne, and the schottische, as well as all the square dances. I've studied the patterns in a book I have. They are very simple."

Pa asked with a smile, "Have you ever tried them with a real, live lady in your arms, Mike?"

"No, I haven't. That isn't necessary." Michael looked sourly at me, though I hadn't said anything. "Dancing has to be easy. So many danged-fool galoots seem to do it well enough."

"Yep," I said to him, "after you've gone to the operetta with Miss Cantrell, you ought to invite her to the square dance at the Osborne Valley Grange Hall coming up in July."

"Maybe I will, maybe I will. Don't keep rushing me so much, Lacy."

"I hope you've taken note of how happy Hector is these days," I added.

"I have. He acts like he's gone crazy. He even grins when he's driving the hearse. Folks don't like that."

"Well, you two have a chance to be just as happy as Hector," I said. "All one of you has to do is marry Miss Cantrell. After all, she doesn't know as much about you as I do. I wouldn't have either one of you."

Michael pointed his table knife at me. "I pity the poor galoot who does marry you. If you don't poison him with your cooking, you'll stab him to death with your tongue. You aren't one bit like Ma, Lacy."

I said, "No, I won't put up with everything she put up with."

"I suppose it might be because you aren't truly a Bingham."

"Michael," said Pa warningly.

I went on. "Neither was Ma a true Bingham. By birth she was a Terwilliger, but she spent all her life making Binghams happy."

"Amen to that," came from Pa. "Now let's quit this family squabbling. What's for dessert, Lacy?"

"Pa, there isn't any. I tried to make an upside-down cake in the iron skillet. I used a whole can of sour red cherries, but I couldn't get the cake out of the pan. It got stuck. The pan's soaking out on the back porch right now."

"Oh, Lord," said Michael with a sigh. "So that's what burned tonight."

✿ ✿ ✿

Pa came out into the kitchen later that night to say, "Lacy, I'm sure sorry we can't get a housekeeper. It ain't right that somebody young as you are has to take over for all of us. I don't think Ma expected things to turn out that way."

I swung around from the dishpan in the sink. "Pa, I wouldn't mind if we were the only ones here. I think I could keep house for the two of us and go to school at the same time, but Michael and Elbert are just too much for me. Even with the laundry being done and Hector gone and Maud here on Saturdays, it's too much."

"It appears to me that you'd like to marry Michael and Elbert off, too," Pa said.

I gave him a sharp look and saw him grinning. "Oh, Pa, I surely do! I want one of 'em to marry Miss Cantrell and move out as fast as possible. I truly do like her. I'd be honored to have her in the Bingham family. I think Ma would be pleased, too. She wouldn't be mad if the boys left home to get married."

"Sure, Lacy, sure. Ma would probably feel that way." He patted me on the shoulder and said, "I'll wipe the dishes for you, Lacy, from now on. I used to do that lots of times for Ma when she said she was tuckered out."

"All right, Pa, thank you. There's a clean flour-sack towel hanging on the pantry doorknob."

I spied on Michael the night he took Belle Cantrell out. Although I'd hoped he'd dude himself up a little bit, I was doomed to disappointment. As usual, he left the house looking as if he were on his way to a funeral. You'd never have known that he'd played his fiddle half through the previous night. I supposed he'd done that to get his courage up to squire Belle.

That same night Elbert went out, too, down to the firehouse to adjust the new Silsby fire engine some more.

So Pa and I sat in the family parlor, waiting for Michael to come home. While Pa read the newspaper, grumbling about how bad things were getting to be in the island of Cuba, I knitted and fidgeted and looked at stereopticon slides of Niagara Falls.

Finally Pa told me, "Lacy, go to bed. Mike probably took her to an oyster supper at the hotel after the show, and then he's got to walk her home all the way to the end of town. He won't be home before midnight. I ain't going to wait up for him myself."

By ten-thirty I was in bed. I lay there, watching the light of the full moon move over the furniture and counting the bongings of the clock downstairs. At midnight I heard Pa come up to bed. Still awake, I heard one and two o'clock strike, too.

On the final bong of three came such a crashing and banging below that I leaped out of bed. I was thinking there's been some mine accident and Coyote Mountain was finally about to fall in because of so many saloons, as several church ladies had predicted. But, no, it was only Michael being noisier than I'd ever heard him before.

He was singing a strange song at the top of his lungs.

"My shirts never see either water or soap
And they have a strong smell like a buck antelope
In getting up parties, I take great delight
If things don't suit me, I soon raise a fight
I go get my pistol. I froth and I roar
And I sprinkle red pepper all over the floor."

When I got to the top of the stairs in my wrapper, I found Pa already there with a kerosene lamp in his right hand and the shotgun under his left arm.

"At first I thought it was a burglar," he said, "but it's only Mike. I can tell by his voice. He must be drunk as a hoot owl. I guess the night out with Miss Cantrell didn't turn out so good. It ain't like Mike to go to saloons."

"Or to drink anywhere else," I told Pa.

Pa grunted, then shouted, "All right, Mike. Stay where you are down there. Don't try to light one of the lamps. Don't move. Don't bust up any more furniture. I'll be comin' down now to help you to bed. Here, Lacy." Pa handed me the loaded shotgun.

Michael called up to us, "I didn't bust anything. I only knocked over a chair before I fell inside the fireplace."

"How about Miss Cantrell?" I called down to him.

"She doesn't want me, Belle Cantrell don't."

I sucked in my breath. What had he done? I

wanted to ask him as he came up the stairs, but the look on his face made me decide against it. He looked like he'd lost a fight with a cougar, not clawed up, but mighty weary.

He stared at me for a long moment, then shook his head. "I can tell by the look on your face that you're busting with curiosity, Lacy. Well, I don't know why Belle didn't cotton to me. I was polite as I knew how to be. I let her do all the jawing, and she did plenty. But finally she shut up, so nobody was talking, and the rest of the night she hardly said a word either."

I had to know. "Michael, did you ask her to the Grange dance in Osborne Valley?"

"Yes, I did. When I took her to the front door, she said, 'Thanks for one of the most memorable evenings I've ever had.' I took heart hearing that, so I asked her to the dance."

"What did she say, Michael?" I asked, as I trailed him and Pa down the hall to Michael's room.

"She told me, 'I'll think it over,' and then she went inside her house and shut the front door. I knew what that meant. She was letting me down easy. She doesn't want to be sparked by this Bingham, for sure. So I went by myself to the Silver Queen Saloon. And *quit* hounding me about Belle, Lacy."

He went inside and shut the door in my face.

I turned to Pa and gave him the shotgun. "I guess it's time to send in Elbert now, Pa."

When I told Maud the next day in her kitchen

about Michael's night out with Belle, all she did was shake her head. "I saw him at the operetta with her. It was *The Mikado*. The story is sure funny, but I never saw him smile or laugh one time. And he never seemed to whisper in her ear either. Lacy, are you going to see Belle Cantrell and find out why things went wrong with Michael? You could use the excuse that you came to her about the nice letter you got from Madame Thérèse in Frisco."

"No, I'm not, Maud. I don't want Belle to think we're a nosy family. She might turn against Elbert, and I don't want to make his sparking any harder than I suspect it's going to be already."

"You're probably right about that. When's Elbert going to ask her out?"

"There's a fire drill and picnic at the end of this month. He won't have to dance a step at a picnic. I tried to get him to take her to the firemen's ball, but he refused. When Pa asked Elbert what he planned to talk about to Belle, Elbert told him he'd explain how steam engines work."

"Will she like that, Lacy?"

"I dunno. I wouldn't, but at least she won't be able to say that he didn't talk."

Maud nodded. She reached down beside her chair and took a folded magazine out of the woodbox next to the stove. "A miner who left town used to subscribe to this, Lacy. He didn't leave any address to send it on to, so Ma keeps it to stoke the stove with. It's a gent's magazine, all about fast horses and styles in men's duds and things that interest menfolk. Here, you take it home with you and give it to Elbert. It might give him some ideas about other manly things beside engines to talk about. Belle sells cloth. Maybe she'd be interested in gents' shirts and cravats and things like that."

"Thank you, Maud, I will." I fluttered the pages, looking at the sketches of gents doing this and that. At the very back I noticed a couple of pages that weren't white but rose pink. There weren't any pictures on them, just words in black ink. "All right, I'll give it to Elbert if I find the right time. He's pretty danged skittish these days and doesn't seem to want to talk to me at all."

Maud nodded once more. "Uh-huh, he's got cold feet. He's scared to go up to Miss Cantrell and ask her to that picnic, I bet."

A whole week went by, and I never got to see Elbert alone. He always seemed to be just going out the door when I started up to him. I didn't know if he'd asked Belle yet, and Pa didn't either. Neither of us dared to ask Michael, who, when he wasn't scraping off key on his fiddle, was sitting around looking like a dark day in December.

Finally to cheer him up, I gave him the magazine Maud had given me for Elbert. It was *The Barbershop Patron's Friend and Manly Companion*. I watched him look through it for a while. Then he snorted and tossed it down on to the table. "Can you imagine any poor galoot in this country lonesome enough for female company to send answers to the women who wrote to this magazine?" And he got up and went upstairs to his books and fiddle.

I was asking myself what he was talking about when all at once there came a loud *clang, clang, clang*, from somewhere below us in the town.

*Fire!* The big brass bell on top of the fire station was ringing. I'd heard it ring three times last year. When it rang this time of the night, there was a real fire, not just a drill. A fire? What kind of fire?

Everybody went to fires in Coyote Mountain. We thought doing so was part of a citizen's rights, though the volunteer firemen were starting to grumble at our coming.

I grabbed my shawl from its peg near the front door and hotfooted it down our hill to Main Street. The fire bell was still ringing, and the street was full of running folks. I headed in the direction they were going, crying, "Where's the fire? Where's the fire?"

"The Bingham place!" a woman shouted at me, as she dodged a horse that a man in the street was trying to keep from shying and rearing.

I yelled back, "No, it isn't. I just came from up there."

"Mr. Hector's place!" somebody else screeched at me.

Hector? His new rented house? He hadn't even moved in yet, because Ophelia's things hadn't arrived from Denver. Well, I knew where that little place was, so along with the rest of the town I ran to El Dorado Street. This was a personal fire, a Bingham one. I meant to be there.

The first Bingham I spotted was Elbert. He was with six other firemen beside the snorting, eye-rolling team of white firehorses and the new sparkling Silsby fire engine.

Hector's little house was surely on fire! Smoke was billowing from its windows and out its wide-open front door.

Now I saw more Binghams, Hector and Ophelia and Pa, standing to one side of the house under a tree. Belle Cantrell and her dentist pa were with them. Belle was holding Ophelia, who was weeping. I could hear Ophelia's voice wailing over all the noise, "I did it! I did it! I dropped the kerosene lamp after I hung the bedroom curtains."

"All right, folks," bellowed Elbert. He'd just been elected fire chief, and he was letting everybody know who bossed the firemen. "Stand back, folks. Give us room and watch the new Silsby work." He called to a big fireman named Bert, "How's the steam pressure on the Silsby?"

"It's high enough, Elbert."

"All right, get the hose to the well!"

Two firemen, miners I knew by sight, grabbed the hose off the engine and ran to the well behind the house.

I saw Elbert take an ax off the engine and heard

him shout, "All right, men, I'm going in now to find the blaze."

"Elbert, it's in the bedroom!" bellowed Hector.

Elbert ignored him or didn't hear him. "I'll find it wherever it is," he cried. "Bert, you come after me in a minute's time while the other men hose down the whole house so the fire can't spread."

I watched Elbert dive into the smoke-filled front door while the other firemen worked with metal cogs and wheels on the engine, trying to get the hose working.

A big spurt of water came out, one great, big spurt that went right through the front door.

That was all. Just the one spurt.

Then the water stopped except for a few drops. The two fireman stared at the hose they were holding. One of them howled frantically, "It's stopped up, Bert. It's jammed somewhere."

"Elbert tinkered with it today," the second man shouted. "Somebody fetch Elbert here."

"Get Elbert!" shouted a third fireman. "Get him, Bert."

"I will!" cried Bert, and he plunged into the front door where the smoke was thicker than ever, so thick now that it made my eyes water.

We all waited and waited. More smoke came rolling out of Hector's house.

Then a fireman yelled, "You, Tom, go bust the bedroom window while the rest of us get the hose out of the well. We'll fill buckets and throw the water through the window."

There was a stampede of firemen to the back of the house. While they ran past, Belle Cantrell came up beside me and took my hand.

Suddenly I was afraid for Elbert. I wailed to her, "Elbert's in there."

"I know he is, Lacy. I know."

We heard the sound of glass breaking and voices yelling as the firemen poured water by the bucketful through the bedroom window. Then came the words, "It's out. The fire's out now!"

Before the firemen had got back to the fire engine that hadn't worked, Elbert was carried out on the back of the big fireman named Bert. Bert laid him very gently on the ground at Pa's feet with the words, "The smoke got him. He ain't dead. He'll be all right in a little bit. I heard him cough when I picked him up."

"Thank heavens, he's all right," exclaimed Miss Cantrell as her fingers tightened around mine.

Well, I had just learned something mighty interesting. Belle Cantrell liked Elbert. She liked him quite a lot by the strength of her squeezing. No wonder she hadn't taken much to Michael. Was that why she'd told me she wouldn't mind being courted by the Bingham *brothers*? What she must really have meant was that she'd like to be sparked by Elbert!

# ≫ 5

# Two Down, One to Go

After a while Elbert recovered enough to get home without being carried on a ladder by the other firemen. Michael, who'd come down to the blaze after it was out, helped Elbert home and up to his room. Elbert coughed most of the night but wouldn't let Pa fetch a doctor.

Michael hadn't caught sight of me at the fire with Belle, because he was on the other side of the big crowd. The moment Elbert opened his eyes and coughed, Belle had let go of my hand, said "Good night, Lacy," and gone off with her pa.

While I lay abed listening to Elbert cough the smoke out of him, I thought of the joy I would get out of telling him how Belle had acted when she thought he might be burned alive. That ought to put a burr under his tail and get him to ask her fast to the firemen's picnic. Oh, I could hardly wait to talk to him privately at breakfast.

But when he came down, pale as buttermilk, he didn't give me a chance to say anything. He drank his coffee down in one gulp and said, "I don't understand what went wrong with the hose last night. I've got to go down to check." And, pushing back his chair, he said good-bye and went out the back door.

I didn't see him again until late afternoon when I was preparing supper. He came in through the back door, wearing the longest face I'd seen on him since the day Ma had passed away.

"Elbert, are you all right?" I asked.

"No, I ain't. Not one bit right, Lacy, but it ain't my health." He coughed. "I'm going up to my room now."

As he went through the kitchen door into the dining room, I called, "Did you find out what was wrong with the fire engine, Elbert?" I didn't get an answer; he was already gone.

Not until I yelled, "Elbert, supper's on the table," did he come down. His face was still the color of buttermilk and just as long as it had been earlier. When he sat down at his place, he didn't look at me or at Michael, but only at Pa.

"Pa, I'm goin' to ask to draw all the wages due to me tomorrow mornin', because I aim to catch the eleven o'clock train to Frisco," he said.

"Frisco, Elbert?" Pa looked amazed. Michael jerked his fork up out of a corn fritter.

"That's right, Frisco. I'm leavin' town, and I don't know how long I'll be away. I packed some carpetbags already. I don't aim to show my face here again until I come back with something so danged remarkable and spectacular, it'll bug folks' eyes out."

"Elbert, what makes you say a thing like that?" demanded Pa, putting both his knife and fork down.

"I'm sayin' it because of last night. I let the Volunteer Firemen's Association down bad. I didn't do my duty as the fire chief. There was a loose valve that needed fixin' on the hose, and because I got busy with the boiler, I told another man to do it. He forgot, and I didn't check. So because that valve wasn't right, the water didn't come out of the hose the way it should. It was my fault!"

"But the fire did get put out, Elbert!" I said. "And you were brave as could be going inside the burning building. All right, the fire got put out with buckets, not fire hoses, but all the same Hector and Ophelia still have a house to move into."

Elbert coughed, then shook his shaggy head as he began to cut up the fritter with his knife and fork. "When I went inside that house, I made a fool of myself a second time by lettin' the smoke overcome me. But I made a bigger fool of myself when the hose didn't work. It was my job as fire chief to see that things worked right and proper, and I let my duty slide. The town paid a pretty penny in tax money for that new Silsby engine, and the first time it goes to a fire, it doesn't work. And all because of me and my not working up to snuff as fire chief."

Michael said, "Elbert, it could have happened to anyone. Folks make mistakes all the time. People overlook things."

Elbert stared hard at Michael over the rim of his coffee cup. "Fire chiefs ain't elected to make mistakes. The boys at the fire station took it like a joke, but not me. They joshed the pants off me today and off the man who forgot to fix that valve. If I stay here, they won't ever let him and me forget it. He feels near as bad as I do, but he's got a wife and kids here and says he ought to stay. But not me. It wasn't no joke. It could of been a serious matter. Nope, I'm goin'. The firemen can elect old Bert fire chief when I'm gone. He was the hero last night, not me."

Pa, sterner than I'd ever heard him, said, "Elbert, you're taking this too much to heart. It'll blow over. There's no cause to leave town because of a danged valve."

"No, Pa, you won't get me to change my mind about how I feel and about my leaving town. I'm dead set on goin'. I've got to prove myself to Coyote Mountain folks, so there won't be any more joshing and laughing. I don't plan to come back until I've got something to be proud of, to make the whole county sit up and take notice. Maybe you think I don't know how many folks hereabouts laugh at me behind my

76

back because of some of my special inventions that don't work and because of my tinkering."

Well, people did laugh at Elbert's inventing. None of us tried to tell him otherwise.

Hoping to make him change his mind, I said, "But, Elbert, you should have seen how Belle Cantrell acted last night when you were carried out of the house and laid on the ground at Pa's feet."

He gave me a queer, wild look and asked, "Was Belle there? Did she see what happened, too?"

"She surely was. She was right beside me, holding my hand. We were both really worried about you."

Elbert coughed some more, then he said, "That's all the more reason for gettin' out of town. Belle must have thought I was a real fine fireman to let the smoke get me after that hose didn't work. Last night wasn't one bit like that time I saved her pug dogs."

This reaction wasn't at all what I'd wanted. By now I was wadding up my napkin nervously. "Elbert, Belle was as upset as I was. She must like you if she was that scared."

He only nodded. "Well then, Lacy, you tell Belle good-bye for me and tell her to take good care of herself but not to wait around. Tell her, too, that maybe someday I'll try to come back here with something important to show the town."

Pa was on my side. He asked Elbert, "Why don't you go and say good-bye to Miss Cantrell yourself?"

"Nope, I'm not walkin' all the way down through

town to the Emporium to be gawked at by a lot of folks secretly laughing their heads off at me. It was bad enough bein' laughed at on my way to the fire station. I'm goin' to Frisco, and nobody's goin' to stop me."

Michael asked calmly, "What do you plan to do down there, Elbert?"

"Get myself a job, most likely in an iron foundry."

Pa had made up his mind not to fight Elbert's going. I could tell by what he said. "That would be the right place for a man of your talents, Elbert. Be sure to drop us a line and let us know where you're working and where you're living." Pa had gone back to his fritters, which were stone cold along with the fried pork sausages.

"I surely will let you know."

"I'll write to you," I promised. I was tempted to add that perhaps Belle Cantrell would write him, too, but maybe she wouldn't want to. So I said, "And I know that Ophelia will write just as soon as she and Hector get settled."

"That's enough folks writin' to any one man," Elbert mumbled, as he tried to push back the fritter that had slid over the edge of his plate. My fritters were inclined to be slick on the bottom.

While he struggled with the fritter, I watched him and the others. I could tell they felt sad, and though another brother was leaving home, I wasn't as glad as I should have been.

It was two down and one to go, but I took no pleasure in it. Elbert wasn't leaving happily, the way Hector had, which was how I wanted him to go.

I felt even worse when he gave Michael a piece of folded paper. "After I'm gone," he said, "will you give this to Bert down at the fire station? Tell them all I resigned and say good-bye. These are instructions on how to keep the Silsby runnin' good. Bert can do it right. He won't slip up on his duty. My slippin' up will teach him to check things out by himself. It wouldn' be right for me to leave town without writin' down for Bert all that I know about how to run the Silsby."

Michael took the paper. "Sure, Elbert, I will."

"And I'll come right back up from the bank tomorrow morning with your wages," promised Pa. "I believe you're doin' the right thing now that I've had some time to think about it more, Elbert. You never did take to stable work and horses. Machines were always what you hankered after. You couldn't hardly set the world on fire here in Coyote Mountain, could you, when machines were the things that interested you?"

Elbert's head jerked up at the word *fire*. Pa soothed him with, "What I mean is that you could make your mark in the world easier down in Frisco where there are other machine-minded men like yourself. They're the kind you can work with and talk to."

Pa had said exactly the right thing. Now Elbert smiled. "That's what I kept tellin' myself all day. My future ain't to be found here in the silver country. Mike, when you give Bert my letter, will you give him my fire-chief's helmet, too?"

"If that's what you want me to do, Elbert."

"It is. That's what I want."

That was the last I saw of Elbert. The next morning he never came down to breakfast, and I couldn't wait around because I had to get to school. Pa would have let me stay home to see Elbert off at the station, but I knew deep down he didn't want any farewell committee.

At recess I told Maud that Elbert was leaving town but not the real reason why. Maud must have been the only person in town who hadn't been at the fire. She'd been in the bathtub at the time, so she hadn't seen Elbert felled by the smoke or the hose that didn't work.

She hugged me, crying, "Elbert's off to Frisco to seek his fortune! That's wonderful, Lacy. That's another brother gone!"

"Yes, but I wish he'd gone away to get married and be happy."

"Maybe he'll do that down in Frisco."

I stood with my hands in the pockets of my blue pinafore, steadying myself against a pine because the earth was shaking so. "They're blasting again in the east tunnel of the Western Star Mine. No, I don't think Elbert will, and I don't think he'll be as happy as Hector either."

She asked me anxiously, "Good Lord, Lacy, do you think Elbert'll come back home soon?"

"No, I don't think so."

"Are you going to tell Miss Cantrell he's gone?"

"I guess I have to. I'll do it right after school. He wants me to."

"That's polite of him. Then you can tell her about the bonnet lace being Irish, and afterward you ought to turn your mind to marrying off your brother Michael, so he can be as happy as Hector is."

"Sure, Maud."

I went to the Emporium after Mrs. Considine let us out at school and waited by the big glass jars of candy until Belle finished with a customer who wanted six yards of pink muslin and another six of pale lilac. While she was measuring, cutting, folding, and wrapping all that cloth in a brown-paper bundle, Belle looked up, saw me waiting, and gave me a welcoming smile.

When her customer finally left, I came up and said, "I heard from the lady at the lace-and-ribbon shop down in Frisco. She says she could tell from the drawing I sent that the lace in the bonnet is handmade and is called Carrickmacross lace. It's made in only one place in the world, Ireland."

Belle's brown eyes widened. "Well, well. That *is* interesting, isn't it?"

"Yes, but it doesn't prove much." Then I went on to

tell her about the crochet lace that I snipped off and sent back to the lace lady.

"That's exciting," Belle said. "Learning about it will be something to look forward to. You'll be getting some news before long, I'm sure."

I looked at her cutting counter and said, "I have some news for you, too, but it isn't so good. It's sort of about that fire last night."

"Yes?" She leaned toward me. "Is your brother Elbert sick because of all that smoke he breathed in? Has he gone to the hospital in Osborne Valley?"

"No, ma'am. Elbert's gone, though. He went down to San Francisco on the eleven o'clock train, and he says he won't be back unless it's with something spectacular. He was sort of embarrassed by what happened at the fire, and he was even more embarrassed when I told him you were there."

"You told him I was?"

"Yes, ma'am, I did. I told him you were as upset as I was, but that seemed to make him all the more set on leaving right away. But he gave me a message to give to you."

"Did he? What was it?" There was more color in Belle's cheeks than usual.

"He says good-bye to you and wants you to take care of yourself and not to wait around for him, but someday he hopes to come here with something important to show the town. He can't ask you to the firemen's picnic like he wanted to, but I think you ought to know that he planned to."

"Oh, Elbert!" She was shaking her head from side to side.

"I think he wants to impress you most of all." I backed away. "I better go now. I see your boss watching us. I don't want to make you lose your job."

She nodded and called out to me, "Thank you, Lacy, for telling me about the Carrickmacross lace. If you hear anything at all from *anyone* down in San Francisco, do let me know."

"I will. I'll keep on writing to Frisco often myself. Maybe you'd want to write down there, too?"

She gave me a shake of the head, then a smile, and turned away to put back the bolts of muslin.

Four days after Elbert had left, Maud fetched me another letter from Madame Thérèse. Once more the lady called me "Mademoiselle," and in this note she wrote that the lace at the bottom of the gown was a very special sort, circles on top of circles, made of linen thread. The thread could be bought just about anywhere in the world, but the pattern was made in only one place. *Ireland!*

After I'd read the note, I passed it to Maud, who exclaimed, "Golly, Lacy, this proves it. You aren't American at all. You're Irish."

"Not for sure, Maud, though it looks more that way now than it did before. I could be an American baby who was dressed up in Irish baby duds because somebody Irish gave them to my real ma."

"That isn't half as romantic, Lacy, and you know it.

Are you going to tell your pa what you've found out?"

"Yes, I guess it's time now that I've got the two letters to show him. He'll be mighty interested in them, too."

"Why are you frowning, Lacy?"

I said, "You know, Maud, I'm not so sure that I want to know who I truly am now. Maybe my real folks weren't good people! Maybe they didn't want me, so they dumped me onto the Binghams' veranda to get rid of me. Maybe they thought there was something wrong with me."

"Don't be silly, Lacy," she scolded me. "You can't stop now. Maybe you're an Irish princess who got abducted by pirates on the way over here from Ireland, and later you were left on the veranda."

I gave her a look. The idea of being a princess had come to me, and being kidnapped, too, but pirates? "All right," I said, "I'll talk to Pa about it tonight."

After supper I waited until Michael had gone up to his room to fiddle and Pa had lit his pipe in the family parlor. I sat down across from him and gave him the letters from Madame Thérèse.

"How did you get hold of letters addressed to somebody named Mademoiselle, Lacy?"

"That's me, Pa. It means 'Miss' in French."

"Oh, does it?"

He read both letters. "Well, you found out something about them baby duds that Ma and I never knew, didn't you? I got to hand it to you, honey. You're a pretty smart little gal, ain't you?"

I said, "Pa, it was Miss Cantrell who told me to write and where."

"That was nice of her. Anyhow, you went ahead and did it. You showed up dressed in Irish lace that cost somebody a pretty penny."

"Pa, it may not have been my real ma and pa who got that bonnet and dress for me. Somebody else could have given them the duds. But it had to be somebody who was Irish or who had gone to Ireland."

"Or been somewhere where they could buy Irish lace."

"That's right, Pa."

"Maybe that kind of lace is sold in lots of stores."

"No, Pa, I don't think so. If it was, the lady in Frisco would have answered me about the lace right off in the first letter. But she had to do some digging first to find out. Pa, did you ever hear of any Irish folks around these parts back in 1879 or 1880?"

"Nope." He was fingering his lower lip, the way he did when he thought hard. "I never did. Ma and me and our three boys was the first folks here, and for a longish spell the only folks. We never had any neighbors at all for miles in any direction."

"Can you figure out how, if I was an Irish baby, I ever got put into an Indian basket wrapped up in an Indian blanket? And why didn't the watchdogs bark when I showed up on the veranda?"

"Honey, you know that I don't know. Ma and I and the boys wracked our brains about that for years, but we never came up with anything."

"And nobody else came up with any ideas about how I got there or who I was?"

"That's right. We never even found out what kind of basket it was. Ma and I kept expectin' Little Dick to wander by someday so we could ask him, but he never did."

"Little Dick? Who's he?"

"A Paiute Indian boy who worked for us back when the stagecoach station was first built, five years before you came. He should have known about Indian baskets. Well, Ma was the one who called him Little Dick. He came alone around the mountain looking half starved. She fed him and gave him some of Elbert's old duds. Afterward Little Dick stayed on. He had a way with critters and could calm down a nervous relay horse faster than anyone I ever knew."

"I don't remember him."

"Of course, you don't. He left one night without a word to anybody before you ever came to us. He lit out in the dark of the moon. Ma felt sorry for him and missed him. She thought he would come back to us, but he never did. It ain't easy to see into an Indian's mind. Ma believed that Dick's tribe had booted him out for a while and that when he left us, he felt he could go back to 'em."

All at once Pa asked me, "Well, Lacy, what's your next step in findin' out who you really are?"

"I don't know. What do you think?"

"Honey, I didn't even have the wit to do what Miss Cantrell suggested in the first place. I don't know. Why don't you go see her again?"

"No, not right now, Pa. I'll wait till we hear from Elbert. Then I guess I'll go."

He sniffed. "It might take some time if he's going to write us a letter. But then Elbert might use the telegraph instead. Now if we had one of those newfangled telephone things up here, he'd be sure to use it. He couldn't resist that, not Elbert."

The month of May went on, and I couldn't help noticing that Michael was getting more and more mopey. He played his fiddle a lot, but otherwise he moped around the parlor. Pa said he moped over the ledgers at the livery stable, too. The only place I guess he didn't mope was in the Silver Queen Saloon where he often went. But he might have moped in there, too, for all I knew. I didn't go inside saloons.

At last Ophelia invited us to a fancy supper, her first bride's dinner. Pa and I ate hearty of her unfried grub, but Michael moped there, too. He hardly said a word all evening. Sometimes I caught him staring at Hector and Ophelia, who were acting so turtledovey that they made me want to laugh.

I thought I knew how Michael must be feeling: alone, getting old, and on his way to being a bachelor forever. I wished there were some unmarried new-comer ladies in Coyote Mountain, but, according to

Mrs. Rowbottom, no unattached spinsters had come to town for weeks. The man who brought the mail from Obsorne Valley told her that there weren't near enough ladies to go around down there either.

I'd started myself down the road of getting folks married, so I felt I ought to try to help Michael out. But how? I couldn't just snap my fingers and make ladies come to town.

I was just about to give up and ask Ophelia to help me by inviting some single Denver ladies to visit her, when all at once fate, or something like it, took a hand. I was tearing up that gent's magazine Maud had given me to stoke our kitchen fire when all at once what was printed at the top of the first pink page caught my eye.

In curlicue black letters was the following:

*Gentlemen Wanted—*
*to Correspond with Lonesome Ladies*

Lonesome ladies? There were some in other places then. Where? I slammed the stove lid down and went over to the kitchen table with the four pink pages.

They were covered with little boxes with printed messages inside. Just about all said the same thing. The lady in the box was advertising because she wanted to correspond with a "refined gentleman with the object of matrimony in mind." That meant she wanted to get married. Wonderful! At the bottom of each little box was a lady's name and a post-office-box number and the name of the town where she got her mail. Some of

the boxes asked that the "refined gentleman" be between thirty and forty-five years of age, and some
wanted him even older than that.

I was more and more thrilled as I ran my finger
down the pages. By golly, quite a few of the lonesome
ladies were in my part of the world, the northern part
of the State of California. Lots were from Frisco, and
some from Grass Valley and places like Stockton and
Sacramento.

Michael could write to one of them, couldn't he?

Then I recalled how he had tossed this magazine
aside and said he couldn't imagine any gent writing
to these females. No, he'd never write to any of the
lonesome ladies himself.

I sat pondering with my chin in my hands. Then I
scooped up the rose-pink pages, stuffed them into my
pocket, and left for Maud's house. I wanted her opinion on this matter. Maybe she knew what was in the
pink pages and had cleverly given the magazine to
me so one of the bachelors in my house would take the
hint and secretly start writing to ladies.

It wasn't so. She said she hadn't even noticed the
pink pages, only the white ones. We went up to her
bedroom to talk as Harvey was sitting in the parlor
spying. There we locked the door from the inside and
closed the window, because sometimes he crept
around on the roof and listened outside.

I showed her the pink pages. "Maud, Michael won't
write to these ladies, so I think I will have to do it for
him."

"You can't, Lacy. A sister can't court a lady by mail for her brother. What kind of lady would answer a little sister?"

"Oh, I know that. I don't plan to be Lacy Bingham when I write. I'll be Mr. Michael Bingham."

Maud bounced on her bed in astonishment. "Lacy, what if a lady writes back to him, and he gets hold of the letter? He'll be getting an answer to a letter he never wrote."

I pointed at her. "That's where you come in, Maud. You're the postmistress's daughter, and you can keep an eye out for letters. You said you could, remember? You watch for a letter for Michael from a lonesome lady and give it to me. Tell your ma I'll be giving it to him. I plan to ask each lady for a photograph, so I can decide if I like her looks. If I do, I'll try to think about what to do afterward."

Oh, how my friend's eyes were glowing! "Lacy, I know what I can do. I can get you a post-office box in Michael's name in Ma's post office. I'll tell Ma he's taking a course by correspondence in fiddle playing and another one in poem writing and doesn't want your pa to see the letters as he might get joshed. A box will cost you ten cents a month."

"Well, I guess I can spare that much from our tandem-bicycle savings. Wouldn't renting a post-office box for just one lady be sort of silly? I ought to send out more than one letter."

"Sure, you should. How many lonesome ladies are you going to write to?"

"Six, I guess. That ought to give me something to pick from."

"How'll you choose them, Lacy?"

"Well, to start with, I don't want to wait a long time to get their replies, so I'll pick 'em close by. I'll make six copies and send the same letter to every lady. All I'll say is how old Michael is and that he's a bookkeeper and lonesome and likes to play the fiddle and read books. Come on, Maud, help me get six ladies from the pages now. Give me a pencil and I'll circle three while you circle another three. Here are half of the pages."

We looked over the lists for about ten minutes, and then we were done. I said, as I took her sheets back from her, "Fine, I'll write the letters tonight, and I'll put stamps on 'em and give 'em to you tomorrow morning before school. I'll meet you on the post-office steps. You can put the letters into the Frisco mailbag for me, so they'll go out on the twelve o'clock train."

"Uh-huh. Oh, this is so romantic, isn't it? I tried to pick the prettiest names I could find. I got Hetty Simpson and Lucretia Wadsworth in Sacramento and Tilly Standish in Grass Valley."

"I picked Marigold Farnum and Essie Yancey and Veronica Eccles Vernon," I said. "The first one lives in Oakland, but the last two are in Frisco."

"Veronica Eccles Vernon!" Maud said dreamily. "That's sure a beautiful name."

"Yes, I thought it was the prettiest of all, though there was one in Petaluma I sort of liked, too. But six are enough. Please unlock your door so I can go home now, Maud."

When she did, we found Harvey sitting up against the wall, eating gumdrops, pretending that he hadn't been trying to listen to what we were saying. "Don't worry," Maud said. "He can't hear. I tested once just to make sure."

## ≫ 6

# "V.E.V."

Two weeks later, just before school let out for the summer, Maud came back from lunch with such a secret smile that I knew at once the mail had brought some answers to the letters I'd written. I wondered how many and held up my fingers—two, three, four, or five? Maud knew what I meant. She held up one hand and the thumb of the other without Mrs. Considine's seeing her.

Six letters! An answer to every single one of them and all at the same time! This was a wonderful Monday, for sure. I could barely wait till recess and was so excited I couldn't multiply 25.25 by 310.66 when I had to go to the blackboard.

At recess Maud and I went to the eighth-grade girls'
territory down by the creek where no one else dared
come. There she told me about the letters. She'd seen
her ma put them in the post-office box and wanted to
fetch them to me at school, but her ma told her that
there were too many of them. Besides, she didn't think
that Maud should be working as a mail carrier so
often. After all, she wasn't a real employee of the
United States Government.

"Five of the envelopes are plain old white ones,
Lacy," Maud said, "but one envelope's mauve colored.
Ma says it's got perfume on it. She sniffed it when she
sorted the mail and said it smelled of heliotrope. I
told her it must come from a lady poet."

I asked, "Did you see whose name was on that
envelope?"

"No, but I got a quick look at the back of it, because it was lying upside down on top of the others.
I saw purple sealing wax and the initials V.E.V."

"That's got to be Veronica Eccles Vernon. Remember, she had the prettiest name of the six?"

Maud giggled. "I'll bet that's some letter, Lacy, if
it's perfumed. Will you let me read it, too?"

"Yes. You're helping me a lot, Maud, so you have
a right to."

We walked to the post office together after school
and got what was in Michael's box. I thought Mrs.
Rowbottom gave me a mighty queer look when she
handed the six letters to me. I supposed that was
because of the perfumed one. Harvey was waiting on

the front porch of the post office, and as we left he got up to follow us.

"Run!" whispered Maud. "Run to the eighth-grade girls' place. He can't run as fast as we can yet."

So we outdistanced him, hotfooting it to the secret place. There we sat down on the grass beside Coyote Creek while I opened the letters one by one, saving the mauve one for the last.

The first envelope I opened got the nanny of us both. It wasn't from any lady at all, but from a Frisco company that called itself by a lady's name. It wanted to sell Michael mustache wax that would "attract the opposite sex by its sweet but manly fragrance."

The second was really from a lady, but she said she wanted to borrow a hundred dollars to pay some doctor bills before she could begin to write seriously.

"I don't like that one," said Maud. "I don't believe her."

"I don't either. Michael wants a wife, not a money borrower. Let's go on to the next one."

It was from an outfit that wanted to sell him some salve, and it used a lady's name, too. The salve was supposed to cure his corns and bunions, so he could waltz all night with ladies!

"He hasn't got any corns or bunions," I told Maud.

The fourth letter was from a widow lady in Grass Valley, somebody Maud had picked. The widow lady said she was looking for a loving husband as well as a pa to her five kids. She hadn't mentioned that she was a widow in the pink pages.

Maud said, "I don't think she'll do, Lacy."

"No, I'm sure Michael doesn't want to be a papa right away and probably not to five kids all at once. I'll write to her for him after a while and tell her to look for somebody else, because he doesn't make enough money yet to feed seven folks. That's true enough."

Now I opened the other white envelope. This one got my nanny worse than the others had. It wasn't a letter at all. It was only a leaflet using a lady's name that asked him to send a dollar for a phrenology chart so he could find out by feeling the bumps on his skull if he was alluring to the female sex.

"It's time to open the mauve one," said Maud, "but first let me sniff it again."

We sniffed the envelope, then I opened it, breaking the purple sealing wax on its back. What elegant handwriting, purple ink with curlicues, and what a smell of flowers! Yes, it was from Veronica Eccles Vernon, who said she was delighted to hear from Mr. Michael Bingham, who sounded like a "fine gent, indeed" and one she'd like to "meet in the flesh" very soon. She enclosed a photograph, which I looked at, then passed on to Maud.

"Don't you think it's sort of blurred, Lacy? And it's only her head and shoulders."

I took it back from her and held it to a patch of sunlight filtering through the cottonwoods. What she'd said was true. The photograph had either been taken in the shadows or Miss Vernon had wriggled. I could see a smile where her mouth ought to be, and I supposed the two dark spots I saw were her eyes, because they were in the right place in the big blur that was her face.

"Maud, I think I'll write back and ask her for a clearer one. This isn't. . . ."

Maud broke in. "Turn her letter over, Lacy. Look, there's writing on the back of it, too."

Sure enough there was writing, a P.S. and after it a P.P.S. I read both aloud to Maud. "P.S. I was going to Denver to visit my old aunt in any event, and while I was looking at the railroad route and schedule I noticed that my train is going through Coyote Mountain. I'll break my journey by stopping in your fair city overnight. I do hope you can meet me at the depot, Mr. Bingham, on the morning of May twenty-fourth. If not, I'll come to your livery stable in the afternoon once I've checked into your hotel. P.P.S. You'll know me because I shall wear a rose, a white-paper one, on the lapel of my traveling suit and a bird of paradise on my hat."

I stared at Maud as the mauve letter fell from my fingers onto the grass. "What day is it today?"

"The twenty-third, Lacy."

"She'll be here tomorrow!"

Maud nodded. "I guess she wants to meet Michael in the flesh before she really starts to write to him." Maud touched my knee. "Hey, Lacy, I just remembered something else exciting. Tomorrow's the day Ulrich the Unbelievable comes up here on the train from Frisco."

"Who's he? What's he got to do with Miss Vernon?"

"He's the famous magician, the one who's on the posters that are up all over town. The one who cuts off people's heads. Haven't you noticed those posters? They make your skin crawl."

"No, I've had a lot of other things on my mind. Oh, Maud, what am I going to do about Miss Vernon? I didn't expect her to come up here, at least not so danged soon. I can't ask Michael to go meet her. I'm sort of in trouble with him already over Belle Cantrell."

Maud got up and folded her arms over her chest. "Then you'll have to meet her yourself, Lacy! You'll have to play hookey from school tomorrow."

"But what'll I tell Pa?"

"Be sick."

"When I think of Miss Vernon coming up here, I do feel sort of sick. I could have a toothache. I have a tooth way back on the right side of my mouth that twinges now and then."

"A toothache ought to do just fine. That's what I'll tell the teacher for you. I'll say I saw you tonight and you already had it."

Even though Michael didn't fiddle long that night, I didn't sleep at all well for thinking of Miss Vernon. She sure wasn't letting any grass grow under her feet.

Maud was right; I had to meet that eleven o'clock train and Miss Vernon. What I'd wanted was to write to her as Michael for a couple of months and then somehow arrange for them to meet somewhere. But she wasn't giving me the time I needed.

I felt terrible about playing hookey from school. It was my first time and the first time I had lied to Pa about being sick. He believed what I said about a toothache and after breakfast told me to go back to bed with a hot-water bottle against my jaw.

I waited at home until ten o'clock, and then I took back alleys up to the train station, where I sat down out of sight in a corner. I didn't want the station-master to see me and ask why I wasn't in school.

While I sat and waited for the train, I watched the folks of Coyote Mountain passing up and down Main Street. I saw Pa and Michael and Hector go in and out of the livery stable. After a while Hector drove out of the stable in the most elegant of our hired rigs, exercising the new team of black geldings. I watched ore wagons on their way to the stamp mill from the mines, dogs running up and down, and ladies with shopping baskets. Then I saw Elbert's friends drag the sparkling fire engine out of the firehouse, wash and polish it, and then drag it back inside. I wondered if they were still talking about Elbert's leaving town, or if they'd worn that out by now.

After I'd been on the platform for a while, a lady and a man passed me on their way to the railroad freight office. The lady pointed straight at me, gasped, and covered her mouth with her hand. "Zeke, don't that look terrible, though?" she exclaimed.

The man looked at me and said, "Don't carry on so, Bedelia. No matter how bad she looks, and I got to admit she looks real bad, it ain't real. Come on, let's go get the new butter churns out of the freight office and get on home."

Did they mean me? I hadn't looked too bad in my mirror this morning, but maybe I had come down with spots or something since that time. But nobody would be likely to say that I didn't look real, even if I looked bad.

I turned around on my bench and now I saw it—the poster on the wall not far away. Oh, yes! It was one of those that Maud had told me about, advertising Ulrich the Unbelievable.

What a poster! Just full of bright-colored drawings of folks being busy as could be doing lots of things. There were pictures of a lady juggling three red balls at once, of another lady in blue tights walking on a tight rope, of a third lady called the "human flyess" walking on the ceiling upside down, and of a man in a white shirt with a sword hilt sticking up out of his mouth. Those were the little things centered around the main picture. That was of a yellow-mustached man wearing a black suit and a red cape, holding a big shining knife in one hand and something truly terrible in the other, a lady's head. The man held it up by the long, dark hair.

Underneath this picture, printed in big, red letters, were the words:

Delightful Doramae
Done to Death by Decapitation
at Every Performance
Opera House
Coyote Mountain, California
May 24 to 28
Come One, Come All
Gasp and Scream
Enjoy Yourselves

I turned away from the poster, now feeling truly sick. The butter-churn folks had been right.

The eleven o'clock train was five minutes late by the depot clock. During that time I fidgeted, then paced the platform. Oh, Veronica Eccles Vernon, what trouble she was giving me!

Five people got off the train when it came puffing in, three men and two women. One man and one lady I knew by sight; he was one of our town lawyers, and she was his wife. They left the platform right away. The other two men were both dressed in fancy black frock coats and high silk hats. The big one had a drooping yellow mustache. I recognized him from the poster, Ulrich the Unbelievable. The other man, who was smaller and darker, kept very close to him, so I supposed he was someone Ulrich knew, maybe

101

someone who worked with him. I was sure of it when I heard Ulrich, who had a very loud voice, give an order to him. "Elmo, be sure that the equipment gets out of the baggage cars in good order and down to the opera house. Hurry up, the train only stays in this little burg eighteen minutes. Then see that our luggage gets to the Antlers Hotel."

Ulrich turned to talk to a pretty little lady in a long gray-linen duster coat next to him. "Come on, Doramae. Let's get down to the hotel." I saw him take her by the arm. She tried to pull back from him, but he didn't let go. I heard her let out a tiny little yelp, but he kept hold of her arm. In a few seconds they were off the platform, leaving it deserted except for me. I glanced after them and noticed that he was still holding on to her.

Well, they weren't any of my business. Not the way Miss Vernon was. Where was she? My heart gave a leap of hope. Perhaps she hadn't come after all? But just as I was about to leave, counting my blessings, a train worker set two big carpetbags onto the platform, and a third lady came down off the train.

The lady was tall and big. In fact, she was so large that she came through the narrow train doors sideways. She was round as an apple and under her bird-of-paradise hat her hair was as red with henna as a winter sunset over our mountain. Her traveling costume was pale-lavender linen with black braid. There was a white rose in her lapel, all right, but it was as big as a cauliflower. To my way of thinking, Miss

Vernon was almost a giantess. Alas, now I could see why she had sent me only a head-and-shoulders photograph.

Deep down in my heart I knew that Michael wouldn't take to her one bit. I felt sorry for her and sorry for me and even more sorry that I'd ever got myself into the business of writing letters to lonesome ladies.

I knew what I had to do, all right. I'd been thinking half the night, and I'd made up two plans. One was for use if I thought Miss Vernon would do. I would take her to the hotel and arrange for me and Michael to take her to supper there. Then I would say I was sick still with the toothache and go home, leaving them together. The other plan was the one I had to put in operation now. It would be harder to manage, but I had to do it. She wouldn't do!

I walked up to her, putting on a sad and downcast look. In the deepest voice I could manage, I asked, "Please, may I talk to you, ma'am?"

She'd been staring around her, hunting for Michael. Now she glanced down at me, not looking one bit pleased. Her face was pink under its coat of white rice powder and orange rouge circles. She painted. Michael had said over and over how he felt about that. Here was another reason why she wouldn't do.

Her voice was husky and sharp, and she spoke very fast as she asked, "Did you just address me, little girl? What do you want? I'm busy. I'm waiting for a gentleman, my fiancé."

Her fiancé? Well, she *was* rushing things!

"Are you Miss Vernon from San Francisco on her way to Denver?"

"Yes, that's me. Who are you?"

I took off my blue-gingham sunbonnet and held it over my heart. "I'm his sister, Lacy. Michael Bingham's sister."

"Mr. Bingham's sister. I didn't know he had one." Her voice changed. She spoke more slowly in a different, softer tone. "Where is he, my dear?"

"Michael couldn't come to meet you. He's sorry. He sent me in his place." I motioned toward the bench I'd been sitting on and added, "I think you'd better sit down and let me talk to you, ma'am."

Her voice was smooth as silk. "Where is dear Mr. Bingham, dear?"

I hung my head. "Michael's in trouble, Miss Vernon, I'm ashamed to say."

"In trouble?" She shoved me toward the bench. My, but she was powerful as well as tall and wide.

I glanced at the depot clock. I had twelve minutes before the conductor would yell out "All aboard" for the Denver-bound passengers.

Miss Vernon was still silky-voiced. "Now, my dear child, tell me about your big brother. Don't be shy. I'm a friend of the family. He corresponds often with me, you know."

What a fibber she was! "Yes, Michael told me about you last night when I took him your lavender letter from the post office. After he read it, he asked me to come meet you."

"Why didn't he come himself?"

I put on my sunbonnet and looked at my lap so she wouldn't see me grinning. "Because they won't let him out."

Miss Vernon asked all in a rush, "Is he in the hospital? Is he sick? I could go there and nurse him. I can lift up most any man I know."

"No, ma'am, he isn't in a hospital."

"Then where is he?"

"He's in jail again." I kept my head down very low so she couldn't see beyond the edges of my sunbonnet.

"*Again? What for?*" I saw how she was clasping her big white gloved hands together in her lap. They were sure big hands, bigger than Pa's.

"He's in there for the same thing as last time," I told her. "For stealing ore rocks from a mine. Michael gambles, you see. The family livery-stable business doesn't bring in enough money to pay for all his losses in poker and horse racing."

"Poker? Horse racing?" She let out her breath like Elbert's steam engines when they worked.

"Oh, yes, ma'am, Michael's a gambling fool. He broke Ma's heart and the hearts of every one of his wives, too, before they died."

Miss Vernon's voice sounded as if it had fallen down a well. "How many wives?"

"Three. He's been a marrying fool, too."

105

Out of the corner of one eye I saw her shuddering. It was a sight to see, big as she was. After a quick glance at the clock—I still had eight minutes—I went on to say, "He told me last night that he'd written letters to ten single ladies whose names he found in a magazine and asked me to fetch their answers to him in jail when I visit him after school. I'm the only one in the family who'll go near him this time. He told me that he hopes to marry one of those ladies as soon as they let him out because he's sure that somewhere in the United States of America there's some lady with some money who will redeem him from his evil ways."

"My heavens!" She heaved herself up from the bench and looked out over Coyote Mountain. Just at that moment the town rumbled and shook. More mine-tunnel dynamiting was going on. This time it was a good solid shaking that made the bench I was sitting on jig along the platform.

Miss Vernon swayed, but stayed on her feet. Someone skinnier might have fallen down, but not her. "What in the name of all that's holy was that?" she yelled over the rattling of lots of little rocks rolling downhill under the train platform.

"The miners are blasting in the tunnels under the town. It happens here all the time when they need to blow some rocks out of their way to get at the silver ore."

"Day and night?" she demanded.

"Yep, they work by lantern light down there, so

106

daylight doesn't make any difference to them. After a while most folks who live here get used to it, though I don't think anyone takes to being tossed out of bed at night when he's asleep because they're blasting under his house."

"Oh, you poor, poor child." She set her hand on my shoulder. I could feel the weight of her and hoped she wouldn't lean any harder. "Such a brother and such a town! I feel for you."

"Thank you," were my mournful words.

"Yes." She went on faster now. "I do feel for you, and I'll pray for your welfare and for your brother's being redeemed while I'm in Denver. Good-bye, my dear. Please tell Mr. Bingham that I will be in Denver for a long time and not able to correspond with him anymore, but do give him my very best wishes." She let go of my shoulder, turned around, and went like a runaway ore wagon down the platform to where her baggage stood. I watched her pick up her own carpet-bags and hurry back onto the train, pushing them ahead of her through the door, then squeezing inside.

I went to the edge of the platform and watched her move down the aisle of the car to two empty seats and plunk down on them. She filled them both. Miss Vernon's face was a darker lavender than her traveling costume, almost purple with anger. What a big faker she was, pretending to be sorry for me. She sure wasn't hanging around to ease my sad life.

I watched her stare out the window at the platform. Her lips were moving, but I didn't think she was praying for us poor Binghams. All at once she saw me. She reached out, grabbed hold of the string, and down came the shade to blot out her last sight of me and Coyote Mountain.

I turned and headed for the schoolhouse, where I planned to tell Mrs. Considine that my toothache was gone. Maud would want to hear about Miss Veronica Eccles Vernon's very short stay in town. I wished she could have been there. She would have enjoyed seeing Ulrich the Unbelievable, Elmo, and Mrs. Ulrich, the lady named Doramae.

Before I left the platform, I went back to look at the poster. Yes, sir, Doramae was the name of the lady who had her head cut off so often. She was lots prettier than in the drawing. Pretty and very sad faced.

As I walked past the hotel I glanced up at its windows, thinking about her. And I saw her. She was standing at a second-story window, staring out at the street below. I thought she appeared even sadder than before. Yes, Mrs. Ulrich was a melancholy-looking lady.

That noon, after I'd told Maud about my morning on the train platform and we'd laughed, she asked me, "Lacy, are you going to pick out some more names from those pink pages?"

"No, not right now. I haven't got the heart to after the results I got. I'll keep the pages hidden under my mattress, though. I guess I'll have to hope that some new ladies get off the train all by themselves this summer. We'll have to keep our eyes open, Maud."

"What'll we do if we find one?"

"Try to figure a way for her to meet Michael before some other bachelor hooks her. I'll ask her right off to our house for tea when he'll be up there, or I'll ask Ophelia to invite her. Ophelia would do it."

"Are you going to tell Ophelia about those six letters?"

I bit my lower lip and shook my head. "Nope, she might tell Pa or Hector or Michael. She might not approve and won't like me because of it. Pa would be angry, and Michael would be fit to be tied. I hate to think what would have happened if I hadn't headed off Miss Vernon today, and he'd found out that I'd written that letter. I bet she had it in her pocketbook. If he had seen my handwriting, the fat would have been in the fire. I'm a forger, you see."

"I guess you're right."

"Maybe I'm not only a forger but a natural-born hoodwinker. It sure came easy, hoodwinking Miss Vernon, once I got started. I wonder if I might have some bad blood in me. Maybe I'll wind up in a home for sinful, wicked, wayward girls."

"Oh, Lacy," Maud wailed. "I'd miss you. But you aren't being truly bad. You're just trying to be helpful to your family."

"That's right. That's exactly what I'm trying to do." I changed the subject as I felt better. "Are you and your ma and Harvey going to the magic show at the opera house? I don't think I want to go. It looks dreadful on the posters!"

"I guess we'll go, Lacy. Harvey wants to. He's been real interested in the posters. He says he plans to spy on the magicians. He likes to spy on new folks in town better than old folks. New ones don't know him, so they go right on talking and doing because they think he's only a little boy. That way he sees and hears some very interesting things."

I shook my head. "He's sure queer. He's turning out to be wicked, as well as a handful."

"That's what I keep telling Ma, but she says he'll outgrow it. She says he'll take to reading books like a duck takes to a millpond."

I laughed. "If he ever spies out any unattached ladies, ask him to let me know."

"How's your toothache?" Maud asked with a grin.

"I never did have one, and you know it. But it does hurt sometimes. I've got a tooth in the back that has an edge on it that's sharp as glass."

"You'd better go see Doc Cantrell then."

"All right, I will. Maybe next week."

## ⤲ 7

# A Miss?

I didn't have any time that night to brood over my wicked ways because Pa had made up his mind to go to the magic show. After my dessert of collapsed cake, he told Michael and me that he had three tickets for the fourth row, and if Michael could pry himself away from his violin, he'd take us to the show as his treat.

"All right," said my brother.

I said, "Sure, Pa," even though I felt a bit weary.

The three of us went to the town's pride and joy, the fancy opera house all red and gold inside. As we took our seats, Pa told me he wanted to see if that stuff on the posters truly showed up on the stage.

Hector and Ophelia were there, and not too far away from us were Mrs. Rowbottom, Maud, and Harvey, who, I thought, shouldn't have been up that late, though it was all right for Maud and me.

Well, sir, I had to admit that all of that stuff I'd seen on the poster appeared in front of our amazed eyes that evening.

Mr. Ulrich the Unbelievable was some magician, and Mr. Elmo was some helper, and little Mrs. Ulrich knew her onions, too. The three of them did things behind the kerosene-lantern footlights that made everybody in the opera house gasp over and over.

Mr. Ulrich did remarkable feats with what appeared to be an ordinary high silk hat. He broke eggs into it and then took out a baked cake, and afterward he reached down and brought out three doves that flew all over the theater until Mr. Elmo whistled them back and they came to light on each of his shoulders and the top of his head.

My, but Mrs. Ulrich was talented! She juggled four balls and some little Indian clubs. Then, carrying a scarlet parasol, she danced on a tightrope stretched across the stage and out over the audience. She passed right over our heads in the fourth row. I thought she looked just beautiful in her silver-spangled white tights and white slippers, even though some people considered tights shocking. After she'd danced back to the stage on the rope, smiling all the time, she went behind a curtain and came back in red boots laced up to her knees. As everyone held his breath, she walked up the wall alongside the stage and then slowly and carefully walked across the ceiling as the human flyess. I didn't like that part one bit and could hardly bear to watch her.

"Oh, she'll be all right," I heard a man behind us saying. "She's got on special boots with suction cups on the bottom of 'em. She's all right if she don't try to run and walks slowlike."

The lady with him complained. "Watching her makes my neck ache."

Michael said, as she came down the wall on the other side, "I don't care what kind of boots she's got on. See how scared she looks, how pale she is! A man assistant ought to be doing that dangerous trick, not Mrs. Ulrich, not a little lady like that."

After that trick came the big event—the decapitation, which was announced by Mr. Elmo. Just watching what led up to it made me bite my fingernails. At first I thought Mr. Ulrich would get right to it when he walked out onto the stage with a sword in one hand. Mr. Elmo and Mrs. Ulrich stood far from him, one at each end of the stage. I watched Mr. Ulrich take off his red cape, black coat, and cravat.

He called out, "Will some gentleman from the audience come up here to touch this sword of mine and tell all of you that there's no trickery about it, and that it is only a regular, everyday blade."

Nobody moved. Finally the mayor, who did all sorts of odd jobs around town, got out of his seat and went to the stage to handle the sword. He tried to shove its blade back into the hilt, but he couldn't ram it down no matter how hard he tried. He shouted, "What this magic man says is true, my fellow citizens of Coyote Mountain. This is a plain old sword, like any other you ever saw."

"Excellent. Thank you, Mr. Mayor," came from the magician, who opened his shirt to the waist so we could admire his manly, but hairless, chest.

Then he grabbed the sword with both hands, flung his head way back, and put the blade into his mouth. While I watched, gagging, he slowly pushed the blade down inside him until only the hilt stuck up out of his mouth.

Pa said to Michael, "I wonder when that thing's going to hit bottom? Now that trick is something to see."

"Yep," Michael agreed.

I whispered to Michael, "I bet that's what he uses to cut off his wife's head."

Michael didn't say anything, but I heard him grunt a little as Ulrich inch-by-inch hauled the sword back up out of his innards.

Something very strange happened afterward. Mrs. Ulrich left the stage, darted behind the curtain, and came back with a fiddle and a bow. She put the fiddle under her chin and started to play beautiful, tuneful music, sad and yet fiery, like Gypsy music.

I looked at Michael. He was sitting up in his seat with his mouth wide open, staring at her as if he couldn't believe ladies could fiddle. She played for a time, but when Ulrich pulled the sword out of his insides, he called to her, "Stop that, Doramae." She didn't stop, though. She went on playing. Her refusal seemed to make him mad. The third time she refused, he tried to grab the fiddle, but she ran away, fiddling faster and faster. They circled the stage until he finally caught her. Then he took her fiddle away and gave it to Mr. Elmo, who carried it backstage.

Mr. Ulrich shook his wife and went on shaking her until Mr. Elmo came back, pushing a great wooden crate onto the stage. It was a real crate; we could hear it scraping on the floor. Ulrich grabbed the lady and wrestled her down, so she was lying on top of the crate facedown. I heard Michael mutter angrily and Pa grunt. Mr. Elmo took a white cloth out of his breast pocket, held it up for the audience to see, then threw it over the lady's head.

To my horror and amid shriekings and gaspings, Mr. Ulrich began to saw on the place where the lady's head was under the cloth.

The deed didn't take him long at all. After only a couple of strokes, he jerked away the cloth and, reaching down, picked up her cut-off head. I couldn't believe my eyes as he carried it around the stage. How dreadful! He then covered it with a cloth and put it beside the rest of her, down where her knees were. He lit himself a cheroot, which I thought very heartless, whisked the cloth off her head again, and put the cheroot into her mouth. In a while the cheroot started glowing red, and tobacco smoke began to come out of her mouth. Ulrich let out a shout of fright and once more threw the cloth over his wife's head. He took it off again in a minute, picked up the head and took it to where her shoulders were, and threw that same white cloth down over her neck. As he stuffed the head under the cloth, he seemed to be trying to screw it back onto her neck.

A lady in the audience cried out, "Oh, my God, he's killed her!"

Pa said, "She's a bit late in sayin' that."

But I wasn't listening to them. Stuck to my seat in horror, I was watching Ulrich the Unbelievable as he drew off the cloth and stepped back, yelling, "Hey, presto!"

Up from the top of the crate rose Mrs. Ulrich, all of her in one piece, smiling, bowing, and throwing kisses to the audience.

"She made it!" bellowed a miner somewhere to my right.

"Hurray, hurray!" everybody shouted. The clapping started and went on and on because the show was over.

As Pa and Michael and I came out onto the front steps, Pa said, "By the great Lord Harry, that was something to see!"

"I don't take to all the parts of it, though," Michael told him. "Any lady who can fiddle that well ought to be saved from things like ceiling-walking. She shouldn't do anything on stage but fiddle. That was enough."

116

"Not everybody's so taken with the fiddle as you are, Mike. The town liked the whole show."

"I'm going to the Silver Queen Saloon," said Michael.

Pa said, "All right, you do that. Lacy and me are goin' home, ain't we, honey?"

"Yes, Pa, I'm tired."

"Is that tooth botherin' you?"

"No, not right now."

"That's good."

While he and I walked home together, I hoped that the day I'd put in wouldn't give me bad dreams, what with all my wild fibbing. It had been a day to remember for the rest of my life, all right.

Harvey Rowbottom was sitting on the schoolhouse steps when Maud and I came out together the next afternoon. We stood on the top step and looked down on him.

I asked her in a whisper, "Shall we run to the eighth-grade girls' place now and get rid of him?"

"No, it's too close, and he might follow us. Maybe we'll want to use it during the summer. After all we won't be able to next fall. Then the new eighth-grade girls get it for their own."

"I know." I sighed. I'd miss this red-painted schoolhouse and the creek and Mrs. Considine. But I couldn't stop the clock that was pushing me hour by hour into growing up. "Why don't you ask Harvey what he's doing here?" I suggested. "Maybe your ma sent him. Maybe we got a letter from Elbert?"

"All right." Maud raised her voice. "What're you doing here, Harvey?"

He got up, fists ready, as two first-grade boys passed him with their fists up, too. They would have hit him for sure if Maud hadn't been there, and he would have hit them back.

Harvey growled at his sister after the boys had run down onto the playground. "I been up at the hotel, Maud, sittin' on the porch outside the place folks eat in."

"He means the dining room," Maud explained. "He was eavesdropping. It's his latest favorite place to do that. What did you hear?" she asked, as she came down the steps. "Was the magician we saw last night around?"

"You bet, Maud." Harvey's eyes were very bright. "The magic man, the one who cuts off heads, talks real, real loud. He was eating lunch with that lady who gets it done to her." Harvey paused. "He makes her eat carrots and her peas just the way Ma does to me. He had apple pie for his dessert and so did the other little man, but the head-cutter-offer wouldn't let the lady have pie or anythin' else, though he had two pieces."

Maud and I looked at one another over Harvey's head. I wanted to laugh. "Maybe he thinks she might get too fat," I said. "What did she say to him?"

118

Harvey shook his long curls. "Nothing at all. I never heard her say anything all the time she was eating. It was like she knowed I was out there listening."

Harvey and his peas and carrots and pie! I told him, "That lady is Mrs. Ulrich. Mr. Ulrich's probably just looking out for her health. Ma Bingham was always a great one for our eating vegetables, not just desserts."

Harvey stood his ground. "Lacy, the magic man didn't say 'eat your peas and carrots' in a nice way. He didn't say 'eat them because they're good for you.' What he said was, 'Eat 'em, Doramae. I paid for 'em. They came along with the dinner, and the pie and cake don't. They're extra.'"

Then I remembered how Ulrich the Unbelievable had pulled that lady down off the platform and how she'd looked when I'd glanced up and seen her in the hotel window.

But I had more important matters to think about. "I've got to go home now and start supper for Pa and Michael," I told Maud and Harvey. "Afterward I've got a letter to write to that lady in Grass Valley. You know the one I mean, Maud."

She winked at me. "The one with five kids?"

"That's the one. I'll give the letter to you tomorrow at school to mail." I patted Harvey on the shoulder. "Keep up the good work, Harvey, but don't let that head-cutter-offer catch you at it."

"He won't. Nobody expects anybody my size to be

spying, Lacy." Harvey beamed at me as the three of us left together.

On my way to school the next morning with the letter in my pocket I heard someone call my name. I turned to see Miss Cantrell cross Main Street, and we began to walk along the boardwalk together.

"Good morning, Lacy," she said. "How are things with you? Have you had anything interesting happen to you lately?"

Naturally I couldn't tell her what I had in my pocket or about the letters I'd got for Michael or about Veronica Eccles Vernon, the truly interesting things. So I said, as she fell into step with me, "Well, I did hear from that lady at the lace shop in Frisco. That crochet lace at the bottom of the baby gown is Irish, too. I don't know what it proves, but my friend Maud Rowbottom thinks I'm Irish. As far as I'm concerned, it could be just an Irish baby outfit put on an American baby."

"Perhaps so. More than likely that's it." Belle looked thoughtful as we went along together. "Have you heard anything more from San Francisco?"

I knew what she meant. "No, Elbert hasn't written or telegraphed or anything. That's like him, though, to put it off as long as he can."

"Yes." All at once she asked, "Lacy, what did you and your father and Michael think of the magic troupe at the opera house? I saw you all there last

120

night. My father and I were in a box at the back."

"I didn't see you there. I liked it fine, I guess, but not the part where the lady walks on the ceiling over my head. I think I'd rather see a gent's head cut off than a lady's."

Belle chuckled. "It's only a magic trick but very effective. I must admit that I have no idea how it is done. I wouldn't like to be beheaded night after night, but Miss Hollister doesn't seem to be harmed by it."

"Miss Hollister?" I stopped in my tracks right in front of the Emporium.

"Yes, the lady who works in the show. I met her yesterday afternoon when she came to buy some ribbons for her dressing gowns. She's a very soft-spoken, polite, genteel lady."

"But I thought she was Mrs. Ulrich," I said.

"So did I. I told her that I recognized her from the posters and said that I imagined she must have a very interesting life as the wife of a famous magician. That's when she told me she was Doramae Hollister, not Mrs. Ulrich at all. She said that she would prefer a quieter existence with far less traveling. She thinks this is very pretty country hereabouts."

I'd hardly heard what Belle was saying. Here was a single lady, a miss, not another missus. But how was I going to get Michael to meet this new lady?

I told Belle good-bye, and she went in to her job. In school I spent my time pondering how to get Miss

Hollister and Michael together when she was going to be in town only a couple of days.

"What's the matter with you, Lacy?" Maud asked me at morning recess. When I told her what was wrong and gave her the letter to be mailed to Grass Valley, she sighed along with me. "Sure as shooting, this Miss Hollister is going to get away from us, Lacy. I can't figure any way to nail her either, not when she's so temporary."

I had to hurry home that afternoon and heat up the oven to bake potatoes for supper, so I didn't walk to the post office with Maud. That was one of the luckiest things that ever happened to me.

Right after I left school I ran smack-dab into Harvey. He was coming down Bingham Street toward me with a bouquet of sweet peas and roses in one hand and a wide smile on his face.

"Where'd you get those, Harvey?" I asked him. "Is it your ma's birthday?"

"Nope. I went and got 'em from the Chinese man who sells carrots and pole beans. He sells flowers, too. A man give me fifteen cents to buy them. Ten cents for the flowers and a nickel for me to carry 'em to somebody else."

"Who? What somebody, Harvey?" He looked so solemn and important I wanted to laugh.

"That lady who gets her head cut off."

Miss Hollister! Some man was sending her flowers. The town's crowd of bachelors must have learned she wasn't Mrs. Ulrich. "Harvey, who was the gent?"

"I dunno." He held up the bouquet. "He give me something to put in with the flowers when I got 'em so I did."

I looked down into the blossoms and saw a piece of white paper. I fished it out and read, "From your unknown admirer from Coyote Mountain." Of course, it wasn't Michael's handwriting. That would have been far too much to hope for.

"All right, Harvey," I said, as I put back the note. "You take the flowers to the lady."

Off he went. I followed him, and as I went I looked around to the left and right and behind to see if I could spy out some gent watching Harvey deliver his flowers. There were all sorts of men around, leaning up against hitching rails, driving wagons, riding past on saddle horses, walking on the boardwalk, and looking out store windows. A lot of them stared at little Harvey and the flowers and grinned.

Michael's rival could be anyone here, just anyone at all. I watched Harvey go to the back door of the theater and rap. The lady herself came out onto the little porch. She said something to him I couldn't catch, and then they went inside. I took note that some of the opera-house windows were open because of the hot weather, so I went and stood under one at the back, leaning against the wall, fanning myself with one hand so folks who saw me would think I had stopped to rest.

For a while it was quiet. All at once I heard a man's voice. I didn't have to strain my ears because he was shouting. I knew that voice, too. Ulrich the Unbelievable!

"Here, you little kid, you leave right now. Take those posies with you."

The woman's voice said, "But, Otto, I don't know who sent them to me, and the boy says he doesn't know the gentleman's name. The paper inside says 'unknown admirer.' "

"It don't matter who he is, Doramae. I don't give a rip. Some man paid this kid to fetch them here. I don't want you taking presents from any man anywhere. You know how I feel about that. It leads to trouble. The next thing that'll happen is that this unknown admirer will show up in person. We won't be here more than four days. You won't have time for any men in this little burg. Now, kid, you take those flowers away; take them to your mama or anybody else you want to. And you tell everyone else your age that they aren't to deliver flowers to Miss Doramae, you hear me?"

"No!" came Harvey's loud cry. He loved to say that word.

There was the sound of banging feet and shouting, and all at once the bouquet came out the window in a shower of sweet peas and roses. The back door opened and out ran Harvey Rowbottom as fast as his fat legs would carry him. Without seeing me, he headed straight for home. He'd surely earned his nickel.

I stayed where I was, listening to doors slamming and then the soft sound of a person weeping. Miss Hollister. I stood there for a while, thinking about her and about what I'd learned recently, and then I had an idea.

## ❧ 8

# A Hero in the Family

Taking a deep breath, I went up and rapped on the back door. Miss Hollister opened it, red-eyed but still pretty in a white-muslin shirtwaist with a huge black-silk bow tying back her hair.

"Yes, what can I do for you?" she asked.

"My name's Lacy Bingham. I'm a friend of the lady at the Emporium, the one who sold you some ribbons. She told me you thought this was pretty country up here in the hills. Well, my family owns a livery stable, and I came to ask you if you'd like to go out riding with me tomorrow. It won't cost you anything. Us Binghams would like to do it for a visitor. We thought you were just dandy in last night's show."

"Riding? Out in the country for a while? Oh, yes, I think that would be fine. Just you and myself?"

"That's right, just us. We've got some nice gentle horses that ladies like to ride. I've been a guide for my pa for single-lady riders for quite a while now. I know the safe places to go." Everything was true; I was a good rider. "You can ride a horse, can't you? I guess if you can walk on tightropes and on ceilings you can do that."

"Yes, I can, and I'd like very much to go riding with you, Lacy Bingham. Come inside, please."

I followed her down a hall with closed rooms on each side and up to a door, where she knocked.

"Come in," called Ulrich's voice.

Oh, I hadn't bargained on him. He was sitting and talking to the dark-haired man named Elmo. Mr. Elmo was pulling things out of a big tin trunk on the floor. "What is it, Doramae?" Ulrich snapped. "Who's this kid now?"

"Miss Bingham. Her family has a livery stable. She's come to ask me to go riding with her."

"For tomorrow morning, mister," I put in. "It won't cost her anything. It's a treat from us Binghams."

"How many other folks will be going with you?" he asked me.

"Nobody, just her and me."

"Otto, I'd like to do it. It would be nice to see the countryside around here, not just the inside of a hotel or a stuffy theater."

As he lit a cigar, he said, "All right, but you be back

by one, Doramae. You hear me? You should get some time to rest up in the hotel room before the show. You didn't fiddle as good as usual last night, you know." He turned his head away to call out, "No, no, Elmo, not the long, blond wig. The short, black one, that's the one I want to see."

Miss Hollister and I went out together, and she shut the door behind her. "Where is your livery stable, dear?" she asked.

"Across the street and down a ways. You can tell by the sign on it, Jonah Bingham and Sons. It's the only livery stable in town." I paused. "My friend Belle Cantrell, who sold you the ribbons, said you were Miss Hollister. That's right, isn't it? You aren't married to one of those gents in there?" Could she be a secret wife?

She set my mind at ease right away. "No, I'm not. It isn't a stage name, but my real name. I'm not married to anyone."

I held back the word *good* and said instead, "I'll meet you at the stable at ten o'clock." That was the right hour in my estimation. It ought to give me time.

Miss Hollister came to the livery stable right on the dot the next morning. I was at the door to meet her with two horses, already saddled and bridled. I took the pinto; the gray was for her. Oh, but she was elegantly turned out in a riding costume of a long skirt, black jacket, and a black hat with a veil behind. I figured she'd be fancy, so I had put a side-saddle on the gray while I rode astride. In my divided leather skirt, boots that were Elbert's when he was a boy, and one of Pa's old felt hats, I looked like a ragamuffin.

I could tell by the way Pa looked that he admired her outfit, too. He helped her mount and then complimented her on her work in the magic show. Afterward, we rode out together. As we went out the wide horses' door, she asked, "I see by the sign that it is *and Sons*. Where are the sons?"

Of course, I knew where they were, but I answered carefully. "Well, Hector, the only one who's married, is the oldest. He drives the hearse we rent to the town undertaker, and today he went to a funeral at nine o'clock. Elbert, the youngest one, is working down in Frisco now. And Michael, the middle one, is out delivering one of our rigs to a man who lives ten miles west of town. The man's wife took sick, and he needs to fetch her back and forth to the doctor in a rig because she's not up to riding a horse yet. Michael doesn't generally deliver things, though. He's Pa's bookkeeper and stays in the office most of the time, but because Pa's shorthanded on Saturday, Michael's delivering the rig."

Thank heavens Michael was! Pa had planned to make the delivery last night, but I'd talked Michael into doing it by saying he was looking pale and peaked from being cooped up all the time with the ledgers.

I knew Michael. I knew how fast he rode a horse, and that he wouldn't stay to jaw with a man who had a sick wife the way Pa would. Michael would be businesslike. Right at the moment, though he didn't know it, Michael Bingham was exactly where he was supposed to be, moving along at the speed I had in mind.

So with me leading her gray, Miss Doramae Hollister and I rode out of Coyote Mountain together. Plenty of folks stared at her and me—mostly at her because she was so pretty and elegant—and a number of gents raised their hats. I gave them dirty looks, suspecting one of them to be the bouquet sender, and started to trot my horse to get out of town faster.

Before long we had reached the canyon country that lay around town. First, I showed her Lovers' Leap, the bluff, and the little waterfall below, where we had picnics on the Fourth of July. Then I took her westward into the meadow that lay between two big rocky hills. It was filled with poppies and lupine now. The meadow ended at widemouthed Christmas Canyon, named by gold miners nearly forty years ago. My plan was to show her the abandoned gold mines there and in other canyons.

She didn't talk much during our ride, mostly because she was always behind me. I wished she'd move up so we could ride side by side in wider places and I could ask her questions, but she didn't. I hoped things would go better when she met Michael.

I was longing for any friendly sound, when all at once she let out a sharp cry that made me grab at the pinto's reins to keep him from rearing. Turning around, I saw that her gray was bolting! He came past me at a dead run, shouldering my horse aside, heading off in the direction of Christmas Canyon faster than I ever would have believed. Nobody would have guessed a horse that old would have so much speed left in him. I figured he'd heard or spotted a rattlesnake at the side of the patch. Once I got my pinto under control, I glanced behind me. Sure enough, there was a brownish gray snake crossing the grass. Spooked, Miss Hollister's horse was running away with the only single lady in town.

Oh, no, this hadn't been part of my plan. I had to do something, so I dug my heels into the pinto, slapped him on the side with my hat, and yelled as loud as I could. After a while my horse got the idea that I wanted him to chase the gray. The pinto hadn't even seen that rattler, and he wasn't much upset by snakes in any event. He'd seen them before, they had left him alone, and he'd done the same. There wasn't any nervousness left in him, and I was surprised that there was in the gray. Probably Miss Hollister's crying out was what had started him running, not the snake.

The only good thing was that they were running in the right direction. Christmas Canyon opened into New Year's Canyon and then into Valentine's Canyon, one canyon after another, growing narrower and narrower. Her horse would be taking her down a chute before she'd come out onto a mesa rising up over a river. I prayed that she would hang on as I raced along behind her.

What canyon would her horse be running down when she ran into Michael coming back from delivering the rig to the man who lived on the mesa?

They were going to meet, but not quite the way I'd planned it. If my old horse couldn't catch up with her old horse, they weren't going to have me there to do the introductions. They'd have to meet head-on. At least he'd recognize her from last night's magic show.

Apparently the pinto wasn't going to catch up. He didn't have his heart in the chase. Trotting was more his style than galloping.

The two of them met in the canyon with the most romantic name, Valentine's Canyon. The gray had run out of steam somewhat, and my pinto had gained on him a bit, so I was closing in at least.

I saw Michael's sorrel coming around a bend in the canyon wall. He reined in for only an instant. Then he spurred his horse directly toward the runaway gray. Crouching over the sorrel's back, Michael, a good rider like all the Bingham boys, galloped toward Miss Hollister's horse, then suddenly reined his mount to block the route the gray was taking.

The gray came to a skidding halt and reared, but Miss Hollister stayed on. Her horse calmed down when Michael brought the sorrel alongside. Those two had been stall mates for a long, long time. The gray stayed calm even when I came pounding up behind.

132

Before I reached them, I shouted, "Hey, Miss Hollister, are you all right? That's my brother Michael who just saved your life. Michael, this isn't Mrs. Ulrich, but Miss Hollister!" That would tell him some news.

"I know her by sight!" he called.

"I'm sure sorry our old gray ran away with you just now. When you cried out because of the snake, you scared him," I said.

She turned in the saddle to look at me. Being run away with sure agreed with her. There was pink in her cheeks, and some of her dark hair had got loose under her hat.

"Michael's my middle brother, remember?" I said. "He's the bookkeeper and one of the two unmarried ones. Michael likes to save ladies in distress, don't you, Michael?"

My question was a good one. He couldn't be tongue-tied about it. He'd have to say something.

"Well, of course, I do." He gave me a very queer look. "Miss Hollister, please accept the apologies of my whole family for what happened just now. We're all of us sorry, but there are snakes in this country. Lots of them. I'm glad I was here to help you in your trouble. Lacy's right. It's a man's duty to help out ladies in distress."

"Do you think so, Mr. Bingham?" she asked him. All at once she burst into tears.

He reached out to pat her on the shoulder. "There

133

now, miss. It's all over. The horse won't run away with you anymore. We'll ride together back to town. I promise you won't be frightened anymore."

While she hesitated, I put in, "Michael, we mustn't do that. He wouldn't like it one bit."

"Who wouldn't like it, Lacy?"

"Mr. Otto Ulrich, that's who."

"Why not?"

"Because you're a man, that's why."

Michael said, looking puzzled, "Well, that's true enough. I'm a man. Let me get this straight." He turned to her. "You're not supposed to be riding in the company of a man?"

"No, I'm not." She shook her head, still weeping.

I said, "He won't let her talk to men. I know because I heard him tell her so."

Miss Hollister gasped and swiveled her head to look at me again.

I had to explain. "Ma'am, you didn't know it, but I was outside the opera house yesterday, getting a rock out of my shoe, when that bouquet of flowers the little boy brought came out the window. I got the bouquet all over my head and shoulders, so naturally I stayed around to find out why anybody would be throwing flowers."

She asked, "Then you heard what Ulrich said to me?"

"Yes, ma'am." Here was a chance to learn something, and I took it. "Do you know who sent the flowers to you?"

"No, I have no idea. The note only said "unknown admirer.'"

Michael interrupted. "Let me get this straight. An unknown admirer who sent you some flowers had them thrown out the window by Ulrich, the magician?"

"That's correct, Mr. Bingham. That's right."

"That isn't right, Miss Hollister. You seem to be trembling. Would you like to tell me some more about this Ulrich and those flowers? Once I've scouted those boulders over there for rattlesnakes, we can sit down on them and have a little talk about this business." Oh, but he was being masterful. He was smiling at her, shyly but nicely, I thought. "I saw your magic show last night, miss. I think you're a dandy little fiddler. I fiddle a bit, myself."

I added, "He does, Miss Hollister, though he isn't very good. We all liked the show, but not the part where you walked on the ceiling."

"Yes," Miss Hollister said in a little voice. "That very act killed my older sister ten years ago. She was truly Mrs. Ulrich."

"Lord!" exploded Michael. "And you're the one doing it now!" He swung off the sorrel, handed its reins to me, then headed for the boulders after taking his rifle out of its saddle scabbard.

"Does your brother always go around armed?" Miss Hollister asked me.

"No, he doesn't even have a pistol when he's in town the way some of the menfolks do. He doesn't hold

135

with 'em unless he needs to protect himself from snakes or mountain lions. There are mountain lions in the timber country beyond here on the mesa, but I wasn't going to take you out of these canyons. Besides, I figured you'd meet up with Michael somewhere, because he delivered the horse and rig to folks out this way." I went on talking fast, trying to say as much as I could to build Michael up before he came back. "He's steady as a rock and he doesn't drink hardly at all and he never gambles and he loves music and he has a very tender heart. You have no idea how much he didn't like watching you be the human flyess last night or how much he liked your music. He really thought a man should do that trick, not a lady."

"Why, that's most kind of Mr. Bingham. He seems to be a very nice man," she said softly.

"He sure is. He'd make some lady the best husband in this whole county. Can you cook, Miss Hollister?"

"Yes, I can. I helped keep house for Mr. Ulrich when we were working at the theaters in San Francisco. He has a house of his own there. Look, your brother's coming back now."

I said, "Good, he didn't have to blast any rattlers. He doesn't even like shooting them, he's so gentle-natured."

I could tell by her little smile that I'd said the right thing. So now I told her, "Some people say that my brother Elbert is the handsomest of the single ones, but I say Michael is." I had to admit that he looked better today than I'd seen him in a long time. He wasn't dressed in his bookkeeper's black suit and vest but in an old green-flannel shirt of Hector's and a wide-brimmed, black felt hat. "His hair is naturally curly, too."

"You don't resemble him, do you?"

"That's because I'm not a real Bingham. I was left on their veranda as a baby in some Irish baby duds, in an Indian basket. I don't know who I am."

"Heavens!" she exclaimed, taking her eyes from Michael and turning them on me, wide as could be.

Michael came up grinning. He amazed me by giving me the reins of her gray, too, and holding up his arms to help her down. Slowly he set her on her feet as if he liked doing it. Then he said something very gallant. "Why, you don't weigh more than a sack of oats, Miss Hollister!"

"Thank you, Mr. Bingham," was her polite reply.

I got off my pinto by myself, and I led the three horses to where Michael had seated her like a princess on a flattop boulder. My, but he was being very masterful now.

I heard him ask, "Now tell me about the flowers and that dangerous stunt."

She sighed. "Mr. Bingham, I shouldn't trouble you with my problems."

"You surely should. You're afraid you'll fall, aren't you?"

"Oh, yes, I am. Everytime I do the act I pray all the way through it. It didn't frighten my sister, but it does me. I was raised by her and Mr. Ulrich. She and I lost our parents before she married him, and she was most kind to me. I became part of the act at a very early age. We traveled a good deal. As a child, I used to bring Mr. Ulrich the sword he swallowed and play the violin, too, because he found out that I had a natural talent for music. My sister taught me to read and write as I never really went to school. Those days I got along well with Mr. Ulrich, and for a long time after my sister died, too, although I never did take much to being decapitated. But, two years ago, Otto decided to bring back the human-flyess stunt and wanted me to do it, because a lady made it more thrilling to an audience than a man." She was weeping again.

"Go on," ordered Michael, while my pinto began to nibble at the top of my hat. His worst fault was nibbling on things near him.

Miss Hollister continued. "That trick is very popular. Mr. Ulrich knows I hate it, but he says that if I'm careful, it's safe enough. He says I owe it to him to keep on with it because he's fed and clothed me all these years. Last month he hinted that he thought he and I should get married so he could take care of me forever. After all, I'm only his sister-in-law and no relation to him. He says if we marry, I'd always be part of the magic show and in the Ulrich family, but I think of him more as a father than anything else. Sometimes he's kind to me, and I do owe him a great deal, you know. When my sister died, he could have sent me to an orphanage, but he didn't."

"Nope." Michael snorted. "He worked you. You were

useful to him. I doubt if lady fiddlers grow on trees. And he doesn't want you to see or talk with any other men?"

"No, only with him or with Mr. Elmo, his helper. He lets me talk with ladies, though. That's why I went out riding with your sister here when she invited me. She's such a sweet child." She smiled at me over her handkerchief.

Me, a sweet child? That made me blush and think of Veronica Eccles Vernon and the widow in Grass Valley.

Miss Hollister went on. "No, Mr. Bingham, your sister is quite right. I should ride back to town with her, just the two of us together. Otto wouldn't like seeing you with us. He says that if I get mixed up with other men in the towns we tour, it could lead to much trouble."

Michael got up. "That wouldn't suit me. Suppose your horse ran away with you again? This time you could fall off and get hurt. You're under the protection of us Binghams now, and if you have any bad trouble with that magician, you come to us any hour of the day or night."

I thought he was being wonderful. "You bet, Miss Hollister. Our pa was the first person to settle in Coyote Mountain. In fact, the town grew up around him and Ma Bingham, who's dead now. Pa's a good friend of the sheriff and the mayor, and so is Michael here."

"Thank you, dear." Miss Hollister put her gloved

hand on my shoulder. "Your stepmother must have felt blessed in having you as a daughter."

"She sure did, ma'am," Michael said. "Ma doted on Lacy. She always hankered after a baby girl, and Lacy sure fit the bill for her."

A compliment from one of my brothers! I turned pink with pleasure as I mounted my horse and Michael helped Miss Hollister up onto hers. He rode beside her down the narrow canyons toward our town while I trailed behind. I could hear the sound of his voice and of hers, but not what they were saying. He certainly wasn't one bit shy with Miss Hollister. I figured the excitement of being a hero had taken the curb rein off his tongue.

I was a distance behind them as we rode into town, and I saw Michael point toward our house up on the hill. Yes, he was showing her where we lived; she already knew where he worked. I guessed he was offering her our protection again, and I was glad. What bad luck, though, that Miss Hollister would be leaving town so soon. I didn't think any man alive could get a lady to marry up with him in two days' time—most of all my brother Michael. Even Hector had needed a lot longer than that.

True bad luck hit us as we rode up to the livery-stable door and started inside with the horses.

Mr. Ulrich was there with Pa and Hector. Pa looked sour and Hector apeared annoyed, but Ulrich was mad clear through, red in the face, eyes popping, and fists clenched. "You're nearly an hour late, Doramae!" he shouted. "You're riding with a man, too!"

"Otto," she cried, "my horse ran away with me. This gentleman saved me."

I was too scared to speak up, but not Michael. He said, "That's the truth, mister. A rattler scared her horse, and he ran. I happened to be coming from the other direction, so I could stop him."

Ulrich shook a fist at Miss Hollister. "You won't get me to believe that story, Doramae. You went riding with this girl so you could get together with her brother. He's that blasted unknown admirer, isn't he? He sent you those flowers."

Finding my tongue, I shouted, "No, she didn't, Mr. Ulrich. I did it. I arranged for her to meet him."

"Then this brat is the one responsible!" he pointed at me.

"Otto," cried Miss Hollister, "don't make trouble here, too. Please, don't."

"There won't be any trouble, ma'am," came from Pa. "You said just now, Ulrich, that this lady ain't your wife. So it appears to me that she can go where she pleases and do what she pleases."

"She's my ward," bellowed Ulrich. "I brought her up."

Michael dismounted. "You sure did, to cut her head off over and over and have her walk upside down on the ceiling of one theater after another. She's a woman, not a human fly."

Hector asked her a shocking thing. "How old are you, ma'am? Are you over twenty-one?"

"Yes, I am," she said softly from atop the gray.

"Then you ain't anyone's ward anymore. You're of age." Hector turned on Ulrich. "I don't like you, mister. You get out of here right here and now."

"You bet I will." Ulrich gave all of us a mighty mean look, and, before anyone could stop him, went up to Doramae. Lifting his arms, he ordered, "Come on, Doramae. Get off. You have to practice for a while before the show. Remember what your sister always used to tell you."

Doramae sighed. "Yes, I remember, Otto. She would say 'we have to give a performance tonight.'"

"That's right. The show has to go on."

I watched her being lifted down. She started away, looking at the sawdust floor. Just outside the door, though, she turned and called back, "Thank you, Lacy."

I felt so sorry for her that I couldn't think of anything to say, but Michael cried after her, "Remember!" and pointed in the direction of our house.

I pointed in the same direction and cried, "Me, too!"

Pa shook his head. "Poor little lady."

Michael spoke angrily. "Pa, you don't know the half of it. I offered that lady the protection of our whole family if she wants to ask for it."

Pa nodded. "Glad you did that, Mike."

Hector put in, "She's got mine too if she needs it. That Ulrich acts like she's his wife."

142

"That's what he's got in mind," I said.

"Well," said Pa. "I hope she don't marry that galoot. But it's up to her. We can't go over to the hotel and kidnap her away from him."

"Too bad we can't," I said, and rode to the horses' door to look after Miss Hollister and Mr. Ulrich. She was running along behind him. He was a real swift walker as well as a very mean-mouth talker.

# ❧ 9

# The Wicked Stage

Oh, what a night that turned out to be!

I'd just finished the supper dishes and gone up to my room to tinker with my hair and see how it would look put up when I heard a pebble hit my bedroom window.

That was Maud's usual signal, so I opened the window and stuck my head out. There she was, sitting on the limb of the tree near my window. This time Harvey was with her, which surprised me. Maud and I had had many tree-to-window talks, but never with pesky Harvey along.

"What is it?" I asked her. "Miss Vernon didn't come back to town from Denver or anything like that?"

"No, but Harvey says there's trouble at the opera house. He was hoping to hear how Miss Hollister gets her head cut off, so he crawled underneath Mr. Ulrich's dressing room. Instead, he heard her crying Then he heard a smashing sound like somebody breaking glass, and lots and lots of yelling."

"Him yelling and her yelling, too," Harvey volunteered.

"What did they say?" I asked him.

"The man said, 'You'll do it again,' and she said, 'No, I won't do it anymore, not after tonight.'"

I nodded. "I know what that means. She won't be the human flyess anymore."

"Oh, is that it?" Maud asked. "Anyhow, Harvey heard the magician yelp like he'd got hurt and doors slamming."

"Ulrich got hurt?" I asked Harvey.

"Uh-huh. He yelled 'Put down that vase. I need it in the act we'll do in Denver. Don't you do that, Doramae.' And then he yelled louder like she went ahead and done it."

"Then what happened?"

"More doors slammed. Folks started stompin' over my head, so I crawled out and went home to tell Maud."

"And, Lacy, I ran right here with Harvey to tell you, because I thought you'd want to know after what you told me about Miss Hollister and you and Mr. Ulrich. Harvey and I ran here fast as we could."

"We were faster than she was," came from Harvey.

"Than who was?"

"Her. Miss Hollister," explained Maud. "She wears high heels. We could climb your hill faster than she did. Besides we took the shortcut by the back of the hill."

"Miss Hollister?" I gasped.

"Sure, right down there." Harvey pointed to the ground.

I stuck my head out farther to see the front of our house. Miss Hollister was coming up our hill to the front door as fast as she could. She looked like a ghost in a long white dressing gown.

"Michael!" I cried. "Pa!" I left the window and the Rowbottoms and ran downstairs, yelling all the way. "Michael! Pa! Get ready! Miss Hollister's on her way here to throw herself on our mercy."

I got to the front door an instant before Miss Hollister crossed the porch, jerked it open, and, reaching out, pulled her inside. Then I bolted the door shut. I was out of breath. So was Michael, who'd come storming down out of his room; Miss Hollister, too, was gasping for breath.

"Welcome to our house," I said. "I'm sure glad you hit old Ulrich with that vase. I hope you knocked him out."

"*What?*" I'd sure startled her by knowing about that vase.

I turned to Michael and Pa. "She just ran away from Mr. Ulrich. Harvey Rowbottom heard them fighting at the opera house."

146

Miss Hollister was still in her costume of spangled tights under her dressing gown. Her face was almost as white as they were.

Pa took charge. "Take her up to your room, Lacy. I have a hunch somebody'll be coming after her before long."

I asked, "How hard did you hit Mr. Ulrich?"

"Not too hard."

"Probably not hard enough," Michael muttered.

Pa said, "Mike, you go up and get the shotgun. When Ulrich comes, we'll be ready for him."

"Sure, Pa."

The three of us went upstairs with Miss Hollister leaning on Michael. He left her at my door, and I let her into my room. Then I went to the window and told Maud, "Hoot like an owl if you spot the magician coming up here."

"You bet, Lacy."

"Fine."

Quickly I went over to Miss Hollister, who was sitting down on my bed. "You'll be all right," I told her. She was sure trembling and breathing hard, so I hauled my box out from under my bed and got out the lace cap and gown. "Here," I told her, hoping to take her mind off her Ulrich troubles. "These are what I was wearing when I was left on the veranda thirteen years ago!"

She looked at them, but I wasn't sure she was paying attention, when I heard Maud hoot like no owl ever sounded. At the same time Michael went crash-

147

ing past my door at a run, so he must have been giving the shotgun to Pa.

"Please stay in here till I come back," I said. "If you feel lonesome, you could climb onto the tree limb with the Rowbottoms. No, better not. I'll get them in here to keep you company. Maud can tell you how I knew you used a vase on old Mr. Ulrich. Ask her."

When Maud had come inside and Harvey was halfway over the windowsill, I went to stand at the top of the stairs where I could hear what happened. I didn't go down because I knew Pa wouldn't want me to be at the front door if he had to shoot Mr. Ulrich.

I heard Ulrich banging on the door with his fists, and then bellowing, "Open up, Doramae. I saw where you ran to. Come on out now. Open up or I'm going to the sheriff."

Pa said quietly, "Open the door, Mike."

Michael unbolted it, and quick as could be Pa and he stepped forward to fill it. From where I stood at the top of the stairs I could see Ulrich in his black coat on our front porch shaking his fists at the Bingham men.

He shouted, "You send Doramae back out to me, or I'll get the sheriff onto you for kidnapping her."

Pa spoke up first, calm as could be with the shotgun held across his chest. "What would you expect the sheriff to do?"

"Get my fiancée, my lady asistant, away from the men who abducted her."

"I didn't abduct her," said Michael, who didn't have a pistol or anything. "You won't get anywhere with the sheriff. Miss Hollister has quit your show. You don't own the lady, and she don't have to marry you. She can marry any galoot she wants."

Ulrich thundered, "Maybe *you*, huh?"

"Maybe me. You bet. I'd be mighty honored. I think I'm a better man than you," Michael thundered back. I'd never dreamed he could yell so loud.

Ulrich shouted, "If it wasn't for your father with that shotgun, I'd make you sorry you said that, Bingham."

"Well, don't let me stand in the way of your troubles with my boy, mister," said Pa, lowering the shotgun and stepping back out of the doorway.

Michael didn't step back. He walked through the door and laid hold of Ulrich by the shoulders, whirling him around. He didn't hit him the way Hector probably would have and the way I'd expected. Like everybody else in Coyote Mountain, I'd seen a lot of Saturday-night fighting outside the saloons. Miners were always scrapping with each other.

No, sir, Michael was elegant. He got Ulrich by the collar with one hand and by the slack in the back of his trousers with the other. Oh, but Michael was strong, stronger than I would ever have believed after all that pen-pushing work. He sort of danced the magician across our front porch on his tiptoes, eased

149

him down the steps, and set him onto the ground in front of the house. Then Michael started Mr. Ulrich down our hill, propelling him as if he was a doll, not a man Michael's own size.

I saw Michael give Ulrich a push that sent him staggering forward. As he left, Pa called out, "Don't you come back up here, mister, and don't make a fool of yourself by goin' to the sheriff neither!"

Ulrich turned around then and shouted, "I wish I'd never heard of this little burg. I hope it falls in when it shakes next time. I wish I'd never set eyes on that scheming, conniving brat of yours, Bingham. She started all of this. You folks have ruined my magic show!"

I felt queer. *Me?* Ulrich blamed me. He was the only one except Maud who knew that I was a schemer and conniver.

I was still at the head of the stairs when Michael came running up to me. "Lacy, I'll be taking Miss Doramae to the hotel in Osborne Valley tonight where nobody can find her till Ulrich leaves town. I'll go out the back way now while Pa stands guard, and I'll bring up two horses from the stable. You stay in the house with Pa, you hear? You tell Miss Hollister I'll be coming."

"Yes, Michael."

I went to my room where I told Miss Hollister, whose eyes were as big as could be, what had happened. Then I thanked the Rowbottoms and told

150

them to climb down the tree and go home by the shortcut. They could have gone out the front door by Pa, but they would have given him an awful surprise. Also, they might have run into Ulrich. I could tell Pa later why Harvey and Maud were in my room.

Before Maud went out the window, she asked Miss Hollister for a favor. "Please, don't tell Michael about how we got up here. It's our secret tree, Lacy's and mine."

I sighed. "Maud, I have to tell Pa, and Michael will find out, too. From now on you'll have to come to the front door and knock. This tree-and-window game was fun, but I think it's like the eighth-grade girls' place now that we're so close to grown up."

Miss Hollister had buried her face in her hands. Her shoulders were heaving, and she was making noises, but I couldn't tell for sure if she was laughing or crying. I patted her arm. "There, there, miss. You won't ever have to walk on a ceiling again. Us Binghams will protect you, and once Mr. Ulrich leaves town, you'll be free as the breeze. We'd like you to stay around here, though. We all like you, my brother Michael most of all. He's a gentleman. You should have seen him take care of old Mr. Ulrich without beating the daylights out of him. It would have done your heart good. Michael will be back here real soon with horses, and you and he can leave town together. First, I'll get you a rain slicker of Pa's to wear so nobody will see you riding through town in your wrapper. Of course, it isn't raining, but it'll look better that way."

A couple of minutes later, she and Michael were on their way to Osborne Valley. She was riding the same gray horse and wearing Pa's bright-yellow slicker. I was able to keep her in sight in the moonlight for quite a distance, but I couldn't tell whether she was talking to Michael and he to her. By now he might be starting to court her or at least trying to get her to settle down in these parts. I wished she'd seen him drive off Ulrich the Unbelievable, so she'd know Michael had saved her twice in the same day. That ought to make her feel kindly toward him.

I doubted if I'd be able to sleep that night because of all the excitement. But after I told Pa about Maud and our secret tree talks and he'd laughed, I did manage somehow. Probably the horseback riding I'd done that day had made me weary.

The next day was Sunday. Pa and I went to church, although we overslept and were late. So not until after services was I able to talk to Maud and tell her that Michael had come back at daybreak from Osborne Valley and had gone up to bed before we could ask him any questions.

While I talked with Maud and Harvey listened, Pa told last night's story to Hector and Ophelia. All three of them came up to Maud and me with smiles on their faces.

Ophelia said, "Lacy, when you see Michael, please

tell him I'll send some shirtwaists and things of mine along for Miss Hollister. She's going to need something more than a rain slicker and tights."

"Sure, Ophelia, I'll tell Michael. I know Miss Doramae will be grateful to you. She's a real brick and so are you."

"That's a brave and pretty little lady Michael stood up for," Pa put in. "I hope she stays around here."

"If she comes back, she could have our guest room until she gets settled," Ophelia volunteered.

Pa nodded. "That's generous of you, Ophelia. But it's up to Doramae." He patted me on the shoulder. "Lacy stood up for her yesterday, too. It's my opinion that Lacy and her friends deserve a reward. Climbing up and down trees takes a person's energy, and nothing puts that back like ice cream." He reached into his coat pocket and pulled out a quarter. "Here, Lacy, take Maud and her little brother to the ice-cream parlor and have something good to eat on me."

"Hurrah!" cried Harvey, who was not shy.

I was more polite, and so was Maud. We said, "Thank you," and off we went, trailed by Harvey.

After we'd each had a big dish of strawberry ice cream at the ice-cream parlor across from the opera house, the three of us went outside to sit on the boardwalk. Because Harvey was listening to us, Maud and I didn't talk about my hopes of Michael's courting Doramae.

Suddenly we saw a side door of the opera house open and Ulrich come out of it, dressed in his magician's black coat.

Maud cried out, "Oh, my!" Then she sat bolt upright. "He's coming toward us."

Harvey dived under the high boardwalk. He was scared of Ulrich's temper, and I could see why.

"Lacy, let's run!" Maud pleaded.

"No, we won't. This is our town, not his. Stand your ground, Maud Rowbottom." But my heart was beating fast, and inside I was scared as she was.

Well, sir, old Mr. Ulrich came right up and stood over us. "What have your folks done with Doramae?" he demanded, pointing at my chest.

I didn't budge. "We've hidden her away from you, Mr. Ulrich, and she won't be coming back, I bet. You'd better not try to do anything to my friend and me here, because I'll shout for the sheriff. His office is right next door."

Ulrich folded his long arms over his chest. "I don't plan to do anything. What I want to know is what am I going to do about my performance tonight, my last one in this little burg? It's because of you that I haven't got Doramae anymore."

"I don't know," I told him. "Don't give the show, I guess."

He shook his head. "I can't do that. I've got my helper to pay, and the owner of the opera house needs the money from the tickets he sells for my show. There aren't that many shows coming to this nowhere town that he can afford to miss one. Since you're the cause of all my troubles, I think you and this here girl ought to help me out tonight."

"Help?" Maud's mouth was wide open with shock.

"Us? Help you?" I exploded.

"You heard me. That's what I said. We showfolks have a motto: No matter what, the show must go on. I've always stuck to it and always will."

I jumped up now. "You aren't going to get Maud or me to walk on the opera-house ceiling."

"We can't fiddle or juggle or walk on a tightrope either," Maud told him.

I barked, "Go swallow your sword, Mister Ulrich."

"I intend to!" He leaned over us. To my amazement, he was smiling. "There are other magic stunts besides those Doramae did, you know. I'll pay five dollars to each of you if you'll help me out just for tonight. When I get to Denver, I can get myself some magicians, and a Gypsy fiddler, a real one."

"Five dollars!" Maud and I stared at each other. That made ten dollars in all. That was more than enough to order the bicycle-built-for-two from the Sears and Roebuck catalog.

"Will what you want us to do be dangerous?" I asked Ulrich. "If it is, we won't do it."

"Not one bit." He pointed to Maud. "All you have to do is disappear into thin air, and you, Bingham, will be decapitated."

155

"*No!*"

Maud said softly, "It didn't kill Miss Hollister, so it won't kill you, Lacy."

I asked, "Will it be ten dollars in silver? We don't trust paper money in these parts."

"Sure, in silver dollars. That's all the opera-house manager takes in anyhow."

I shook my head. "Our folks wouldn't want us to do it."

"Keep it quiet then. You'll be dressed up in costumes and wearing wigs and have paint on your faces. They won't even know you. Will you do it?"

Once more Maud and I looked at each other. Then she nodded at me. "Lacy, it'll only be for one night!"

"That's right," he told us. "I leave tomorrow on the Denver train."

I asked Maud, "What'll we tell our folks about not being home tonight?"

"I know. We'll say that sick old Mrs. Tucker asked us to come read to her."

"Then you'll do it?" came from Ulrich.

I said, "I guess so, but if you do anything to us, I warn you, I'll yell from the stage for the sheriff to come up and get you right then and there. The sheriff goes to the opera house every single night, when there's a show, to keep the miners from fighting."

"You won't have to worry. You come to the stage door of the opera house at two thirty, right after dinner. I'll show you what to do. Now where will I find

156

four strong men for one of the special things I plan to do tonight?"

I pointed to the Silver Queen Saloon. "Try over there. It's open, and there'll be some miners around."

Maud warned him. "Hire 'em while they're still sober, Mister Ulrich."

Once he went over to the saloon, I said, "I think we've gone crazy, Maud Rowbottom."

"I think so, too, but remember the bicycle, Lacy Bingham!" She called down through a crack in the boardwalk, "Harvey, you can come out now! The magician's gone away."

Pa and I had Sunday dinner at Hector and Ophelia's, and I enjoyed every bit of the roast chicken in spite of my nervousness about what I was to do that night. Michael wasn't with us. He left a note, saying he was riding back to Osborne Valley right away, while we were in church.

I was pleased, because it had to mean that he was courting Miss Hollister.

After dinner, while Pa talked with Hector and his bride, I went to the opera-house stage door. Maud sat on the top step, waiting for me. "Did you tell your pa about poor old Mrs. Tucker and our being with her tonight?" she asked.

"Sure, Maud. That's taken care of, I guess."

"Lacy, I think I'm scared."

"So am I, but let's keep our minds on the bicycle.

157

Every time you get scared think about how beautiful it is."

We spent three hours that afternoon on the stage of the opera house with Mr. Ulrich and Mr. Elmo, the four strong miners he'd hired, and another little, fair-haired man, who'd come to Coyote Mountain the day before Ulrich. This stranger was a secret helper nobody knew about because he always stayed hidden during the performances. He'd pretended all the time he'd been in town to be a complete stranger to the magician. In fact, he wasn't; he was Ulrich's brother, Cornelius.

Maud and I learned fast what we were supposed to do. It surely was an easy way to earn ten dollars. Mr. Ulrich gave us stage names and made us giggle in spite of our nervousness. I was named Lolo the Clown, and Maud was Princess Serafin. After he named us, he sent us to the dressing room Doramae had used and Mr. Elmo brought in a trunk of costumes and other stuff. We were to stay in the dressing room until the performance began at eight o'clock.

By seven Maud and I were feeling guilty over our white lie about Mrs. Tucker, and we were wishing hard that the show was over. Slowly we got dressed to go on stage, but we didn't take to our costumes. Mine was a clown suit of red-and-white-striped cotton and a bright-red fuzzy wig that stuck way out on both sides of my head. It was decent; that was all I could say for it. Maud's costume wasn't one bit decent. It was all green and violet silk and so thin you could see right through the cloth. She had to wear a pink union suit under it. Along with the costume and union suit came a long black wig and a piece of violet-covered cloth to be worn from the top of her nose down over her collarbone as a veil.

To comfort her, I said, "With that veil over your face, Maud, you won't have to paint anything but your forehead and eyebrows. Ulrich says I have to put on a lot of white paint, so I'll look like the clown in this picture." I plastered on the white stuff and drew a red nose and big, red lips. The greasepaint made my face feel tight, and I didn't like it.

Maud muttered plenty as she tried to get into the gold slippers Princess Serafin had to wear. They were too small for her. She told me, "Mama says the stage is wicked, and now in these duds I believe it, Lacy. Why does the princess have to have such little feet anyhow? I'm sure glad I get to disappear in the first part of the show."

"You're lucky there, Maud. I come last of all on the program."

We had stomachs full of moths as we heard the audience come talking and laughing into the opera house. Finally Ulrich came back to the dressing room and went over with us what we were to do. If we wanted, he would let us watch the show from the sides of the stage, but we had to stay behind the big red-velvet curtains.

Hidden, Maud and I looked on while Ulrich baked his cake in his hat and pulled out birds and did tricks

159

with coins donated by folks in the audience and returned by Mr. Elmo. Ulrich also did some mental stunts, guessing birthdays of ladies and some other things to fill in the time.

Finally he sang out that he was going to show the good people of Coyote Mountain how a beautiful and enchanted Persian princess would disappear before their very eyes! He meant Maud, of course.

Mr. Cornelius came up to her then and said, "It's time for you to do your stuff, kid."

I watched them go to the side where the four miners were standing by a gilded wooden stretcher with a fancy blue four-poster canopy and drawn-back purple curtains. The miners were painted dark brown from head to foot except for short yellow-silk trunks and orange turbans. They were a shocking sight, too.

Mr. Cornelius ordered Maud, "Lie down. Remember what you're supposed to do, kid, and do it fast."

"Good luck, Maud," I whispered to myself.

A minute later the four miners lifted the stretcher. They went out onto the stage with Maud lying on one elbow, looking weary and mysterious.

"Hey, Jake O'Brien, where's your pants?" somebody yelled at one of the miners. "Where's your derby, Owen Jones?" the same man yelled to another miner.

"Behold the lovely Persian, the Princess Serafin!" cried Mr. Ulrich.

Maud nodded and waved lazily to the audience as the miners circled the stage.

All at once somebody shouted, "Hey, that ain't no princess! Ain't that the Rowbottom kid?"

Everybody laughed, but Maud gave no sign that she'd even heard. She went on waving.

Ulrich ignored the interruption, too. He stepped up to the stretcher where it had stopped and pulled the purple curtains together. An instant later, after crying Abracadabra three times, he pulled them open.

Lo and behold, the princess had disappeared! The stretcher was empty.

"Where'd the Rowbottom girl go?" a man cried out.

Another man shouted, "She'll be back!"

"She won't stay away long!" cried a third man's voice.

My, but there was lots of clapping. Maud had been a success! That ought to please Ulrich.

I went back to the stretcher once it was offstage and found Maud cramped and complaining. The stretcher had a double-layered bottom. When the four miners pulled on strong cords hidden in the ends of the poles, the top layer, the part Maud had been lying on, was hauled up by a pulley into the canopy where it couldn't be seen. Naturally Maud had gone with it. All she had to do was keep quiet.

What made her complain was the dust in the canopy. "I could have sneezed in there," she told me. "They ought to dust it sometimes. Hey, I wonder how they knew it was me in the stunt?"

"I don't know, but somebody sure did."

"Sh-h-h," warned Mr. Cornelius. His brother was

161

doing a quiet trick, hauling bright-colored silk scarves one after another out of Mr. Elmo's ears and nose and mouth while the audience oohed and aahed. Then Mr. Cornelius pretended to be a magic painted female head and answered questions his brother asked. This trick was done with mirrors; Mr. Cornelius sat on a stool with his head sticking out of a tabletop.

After Ulrich the Unbelievable swallowed his sword, my turn came to do the last stunt of the evening, the biggest one.

"Good luck, Lacy," Maud whispered.

"Thanks," was all I had time to say. I came jumping out onto the stage, screeching at the top of my lungs. There were some parts of being a clown a person could enjoy. I grabbed Mr. Elmo's long coattails and whirled him around and around. He started to chase me. As I passed by Ulrich I joyfully kicked him in the seat of his britches and did it sort of hard. Waving the sword he'd just got up out of himself, Ulrich joined Elmo. Both of them were yelling, "Lolo, Lolo, you'll pay for this!"

"Catch that kid," bellowed a man from the audience. "We know Lacy. Catch her and give her a good licking. Get the Bingham girl!"

Oh, but there was a lot of laughing after that remark. I wanted to quit and run off the stage, but if I did, there wouldn't be any tandem bicycle, and Maud would be mad at me forever.

The danged show had to go on! I went on dodging

and running until I fell down on the stage as I was supposed to. The magicians caught hold of me. Ulrich shook me the way he'd shaken Doramae the first night for doing too much fiddling.

As Elmo pushed out the same crate, I warned Ulrich, in a whisper, "Not so danged hard, mister!"

"*You* kicked hard, kid. Behave yourself now. Earn your money. Beg me for mercy, then flop down on top of that crate the way you're supposed to."

I got down on my hands and knees and pretended to beg him for a while, but of course he showed me no mercy and sentenced me to die. I lay down on the crate on my stomach with my head to one side. Ulrich threw the white cloth over my head. Instantly I turned my head and shoved it down into the hole that appeared when a panel slid back on top of the crate. With my face in the hole, I looked into the face of Mr. Cornelius beneath me. He worked the sliding panels from inside the crate. I could feel Ulrich sawing away with his sword near my shoulders. No wonder Doramae hadn't enjoyed this trick.

"Make room now, kid," ordered Mr. Cornelius.

Mr. Ulrich cried "Presto" and jerked off the cloth. Mr. Cornelius quickly passed up a wooden head painted to match the paint on my face. It scraped the side of my head as it went by. The magician held it up as my cut-off head. All the time, I was staring into Mr. Cornelius's face, which was painted to match my face and the dummy's.

What a roar came from the crowd! I would have

enjoyed hearing it if I hadn't been so uncomfortable. My neck ached, but I had to stay completely still while Ulrich strutted around the stage with the dummy.

Finally I heard him say, "I'll set this down beside wicked Lolo's knees and have myself a smoke." I knew from our practicing that he was covering the dummy with the cloth again.

While Mr. Ulrich had been showing off the dummy, Mr. Cornelius squirmed around under me, turning himself about and going to the other end of the crate to work another sliding panel in the top. Before Ulrich jerked away the cloth, Mr. Cornelius grabbed the dummy back into the crate and stuck his own head up through the second sliding panel. Ulrich stuck the cheroot he'd had in his own mouth into his brother's, and Mr. Cornelius puffed on it for a while.

Then down came the cloth over Mr. Cornelius's head, and when Ulrich hauled it up again, the dummy head was there once more.

At this point Ulrich put the cloth over my neck and tried to screw the wooden head onto my shoulders. He was sort of rough about it, probably because of that kick I'd given him.

Finally he whispered, "All right, kid. Now!" I heard a soft thud. This meant he'd dropped the dummy behind the crate where nobody in the audience could see it. The next thing he'd do would be to shout "Abracadabra! Hey, presto!" and pull away the white cloth.

This was my cue to haul my head up out of the crate, jump up, bow, and throw kisses the way Dora-mae had.

Well, I tried, but it didn't work! There wasn't space to get my head out. I was stuck, caught by the sliding panel. It hadn't opened wide enough. I realized Mr. Cornelius must have pushed it up too far.

"Help!" I whispered to Mr. Cornelius below me.

Ulrich threw his cloth over my neck again and yelled, "Hey, presto!" for the second time.

"Hang on, kid." Mr. Cornelius slid on his back to me and tugged on the edge of the stuck panel, but it wouldn't move. He took hold of me by the chin and pushed and shoved until I was loose.

All I had time for was to make sure with one hand that the red wig was still on my head. Ulrich yelled "Hey, presto!" for the third time. I leaped up and bowed. That third "Hey, presto" had sounded annoyed.

I ran to the edge of the stage and bowed to all the clapping and shouts of "Hey, kid, you're a good sport!" "Look at the Bingham girl! She's still alive and kicking!"

That close to the kerosene footlights I could see into the front row. There stood Pa and the sheriff and Hector and Mrs. Rowbottom and Harvey, too.

Harvey pointed to me and tugged at his ma's sleeve.

*Harvey!* Harvey had told her about Maud and me being in the show, and she'd gone to Pa and the others, and Pa had come with the sheriff. Was Pa mad at me? No, he was clapping and laughing, too, and so was Hector and the sheriff, but not Mrs. Rowbottom. She didn't look pleased at all. She scowled at me with her eyebrows all drawn together. Poor Maud!

Instead of doing cartwheels all around the stage the way I was supposed to, I went back and gave Ulrich the Unbelievable another kick, a good one in the seat of his pants. That wasn't really part of the show, but because folks were still watching, all he could do was grin and bow to them.

I couldn't say that I'd been on the wicked stage and not suffered for my wickedness. That tug-of-war with my chin was going to leave me with some bruises, but as I staggered offstage to find Maud I knew that wasn't the worst of it. I'd clamped my jaws together so hard that I'd busted off part of the back tooth that had given me a bit of trouble already. I'd heard it snap off and felt a dart of pain at the same moment. My tongue told me that one whole side of the tooth must have broken off.

Maud was going to have to account to her ma for being the disappearing princess and lying about sick old Mrs. Tucker, but I was in for tooth trouble for sure.

Thank goodness, Pa wasn't mad with me to boot.

# ❧ 10

# "Get It Done Down There"

I'd been right about Harvey. He was the big tattle-
tale. I'd forgotten all about his being under the boardwalk when Ulrich had asked us to help. Maud hadn't
figured he'd go and tell their mother, though she must
have known he'd be up to his old game of eavesdropping under there.

Pa had taken my being in the show as a joke. When
Mrs. Rowbottom had asked him to go to the opera
house with the sheriff and stop our performance, Pa
and the sheriff talked her into coming instead. Harvey
told Pa that we were to get five dollars apiece, so Pa
decided to see that things went right for Maud and
me. He knew I was saving for that bicycle, and he

wanted to help. But Mrs. Rowbottom didn't quite agree. Maud got a terrible scolding for displaying herself on the wicked stage.

Still, we got our silver dollars, and the next day Pa told me that the sheriff had quietly escorted Mr. Ulrich and company to the depot to catch the Denver-bound train. This time Mr. Cornelius went with his little brother. Hector and Pa saw them leave, but not Michael, who was still in Osborne Valley.

I thought that Mr. Ulrich seemed glad to see Maud and me go out the opera-house back door that night. We'd been a big success, and he should have thanked us, but he didn't.

That Monday was an exciting day in other ways, too. Maud and I ordered the bicycle from Chicago by letter, and we Binghams got a postcard from Elbert. There were only four lines on it and they didn't say much, but they did let us know that he'd got to Frisco. He also gave his address and said he'd found work in a foundry. So he was still alive.

The third exciting thing that day was Michael's news that Doramae would be staying in our part of the state and coming soon to Coyote Mountain. He was closemouthed about anything else, but I wasn't fooled. The two of them were surely courting. His happy look told me that. He grinned all over like the cat that ate the dickey bird when Pa let him know that Miss Doramae had been offered a room at Hector and Ophelia's.

I would have been even more tickled about all the
good things that were happening if it hadn't been for
my tooth. First, it ached; then it didn't ache. Then it
ached off and on for a whole week.

The day after school closed I told Pa that I thought
I'd better go see Dr. Cantrell, the dentist. Pa offered
to come along with me because, as he said, he'd have
to pay the bill.

While Pa sat in the waiting room, Dr. Cantrell put
me in a red-velvet-and-black-iron chair where I could
look up at the stuffed red fox crouching on top of his
glass case of instruments. I thought it looked ready
to pounce on customers who didn't behave right.

Dr. Cantrell had Belle's red hair with lots of gray
mixed in. "Open wide, Lacy, and we'll take a look at
that tooth that's bothering you." He always said *we*.
When I was younger I'd figured that he meant himself
and that unfriendly fox, but now I knew it was only
the way dentists and doctors spoke to everybody.

He looked and looked and kept tilting my head this
way and that and saying "umm" and "hmm." Finally
he shut my jaws for me and said, "Well, it certainly
needs to be taken out, but I'm not the man to do it.
That tooth has been broken off so bady that it's only
a shell by now. Go out and fetch your papa in here,
Lacy."

When Pa came into the room, Dr. Cantrell said, "To
get that tooth taken out properly so there won't be
any bone splinters, Jonah, you should take her down

to Frisco, where there's a dentist who specializes in this sort of work. He's an expert tooth puller, the best in the West."

"Will it hurt?" I asked in alarm.

"Not one bit. Dr. Friend prides himself on never having hurt a patient. He's up on all the newest improvements in our noble profession. If there's a new wrinkle, he's onto it."

"Can't you do it here?" asked Pa. "I've got some business to tend to at the livery stable. With Michael gone so much now, we're behind on the hay and grain ordering and the bookwork."

"No, Jonah." Dr. Cantrell shook his head. "I don't want to risk it. Get it done down there. All Dr. Friend does these days is pull teeth. He must have pulled thousands by now, enough to pave his office floor. He'll know just where to put the pliers so Lacy's tooth will come out nice and easy and won't bust to bits. And it won't hurt her one bit!"

"Well, well, Frisco, huh?" Pa was muttering, as we went out of the dental office.

Dr. Cantrell was still with us. "Jonah, don't wait any longer than you have to. That tooth could become infected, and then there would be a great deal more trouble for Lacy." He patted me on the back. "I hear tell you and the Rowbottom girl were the toast of the town last week at the magic show. Belle and I wish we'd been there to see you get your head sawed off. Tell me, how is that trick done?"

I smiled. "It's a secret, but it wasn't much fun, believe me. Dr. Cantrell, if I don't see Belle before Pa and I leave town, please tell her that we'll be seeing my brother Elbert down in Frisco for sure."

"I'll be sure to tell her, Lacy. Do you hear from Elbert often?"

"We got a postcard from him a little while back. He sent his regards to all of us, and I'm sure he meant to send them to Belle, too, because I know he likes her a lot."

Dr. Cantrell smiled and went back to where he did his work, watched by that fox.

Pa told me as we went away, "We'll go to Frisco next Monday for sure, Lacy. That's only a week away. I hope Mike will stay put for a while by that time. He's wearing out the road to Osborne Valley with all the traveling he's doing. Well, I guess I know how he feels about the lady." Pa sighed. "I felt like that about your ma when I was young."

I asked him, "Pa, did Ma hanker after a baby girl? That's what Michael told Miss Doramae in Valentine's Canyon."

"She surely did. She wanted Elbert to be a girl. I wonder what else about us Michael's telling Miss Doramae?"

"Plenty, I bet. I hope it's the right things, too. I'm not around to give him advice on how to treat a lady. That worries me sometimes."

Pa chuckled. "If they're right for each other, Mike

171

won't need your advice. Hector didn't with Ophelia, and I didn't with Ma. What to say sort of comes naturally, Lacy."

"I sure hope so, Pa. But I'd like to see Miss Hollister before we go down to Frisco. I want to find out for myself how she and Michael are getting on."

Without any warning, Michael fetched Doramae back to Coyote Mountain that Saturday morning and took her to Hector and Ophelia's house. I didn't see her right away, because she was too occupied moving in and getting acquainted with Ophelia. Michael was acting mighty pleased with himself, indeed. I figured he'd kept her in Osborne Valley as long as he could to court her without interfering folks around—without me, in particular.

He told us Saturday night that Doramae would be receiving a few visitors on Sunday afternoon, and she most particularly wanted to see Pa and me. Well, that was something to look forward to, all right!

That Sunday, after the services, I talked to Maud as usual, not about my tooth that hadn't hurt too much for some days, but about the tandem bicycle and Miss Hollister. Maud promised that if our bicycle arrived before I got back from Frisco, she wouldn't get on it until I was there, too. The back seat was to be hers; the front one would be mine, and nobody else's.

Then I told her that I'd be seeing Doramae that very afternoon at Hector's house, and I promised that if I felt sure they were on the road to getting married, I'd hang my yellow sunbonnet out on the tree limb as a signal. Afterward she and I hugged, and I glared at Harvey, that tattler, who was being held tight by his ma too far off to hear us. Perhaps he'd meant well in telling her about our being in the magic show. Maybe he wanted to protect us, but you couldn't ever tell about him.

Pa and I went off to see Miss Doramae. She was sitting in the little parlor with Ophelia, all dressed up in a gown of pale-green muslin. With Ophelia in yellow lace, they looked good enough to eat, like big sugar plums. Hector and Michael were there and duded up, too. Michael was even wearing a green cravat of Hector's and looking pleased as punch.

When Miss Hollister caught sight of me, she got up out of her chair to kiss me on the cheek. "Dear, dear Lacy. You helped me so much, and I hear that you even helped out Mr. Ulrich later on."

"Yes, ma'am. I had my head cut off, too. But he had to pay me for it since I wasn't family to him, I'm glad to say."

"I plan to stay here in your town, Mr. Bingham," Doramae said to Pa, after she pulled me over to sit down on the sofa with her.

"Glad to hear that, miss," answered Pa, and he went out to the kitchen with Hector and Michael to talk about horses and things like that.

Ophelia spoke for the first time. "Lacy, Doramae plans to give music lessons here."

Doramae said, "Yes, your brother Michael says he'll be one of my first pupils."

I thought the idea was dandy. The way he played the fiddle, they'd need to spend lots of time together.

"I hear that you and your father are going to San Francisco tomorrow?"

"Uh-huh, because of my tooth and a special dentist down there. Pa and I are going to see Elbert, and maybe if I have time, I'll go say thank-you to the lace lady who wrote me about my baby bonnet and gown."

Doramae nodded. "Yes, I remember seeing them. You showed them to me that night I ran away. Why don't you tell me about them now?"

Ophelia added, "It's quite a tale. I'd like to hear it again too, Lacy."

So I told them all I knew about the Indian basket and blanket scrap and the dogs not barking and the baby duds. I finished with, "But after I got the letter that the crochet lace was Irish, too, I came to a dead end. Nobody knew anything about any Irish folks around here or anything else that would help me."

"Mmmm," murmured Doramae, with her hand to her forehead. "You know, Lacy, I have a suggestion for you. I lived in San Francisco and know it well. There *is* someone in the city who might know something about Irish people in California."

"Do you know somebody Irish there?" I asked her.

"No, that isn't what I had in mind. You might go to the British consul and ask him about any Irish people in this part of the country around 1880. Your story is a very strange one. He might be able to throw some light on it."

"What's a consul?" I wanted to know.

"A person from a foreign country who has an office in a big city to help people from his country who get into trouble. We have them in other lands, too," explained Ophelia.

"Yes," Doramae went on. "The British consul in San Francisco is sent there by his government. Ireland is part of the British Empire, so he helps out not only English citizens but Irish and Scottish people, too."

"It's a good idea to see him, Lacy," agreed Ophelia.

I nodded and decided to think about it. I knew that British consuls spoke English, so that wouldn't be any problem. "I'll bring my baby duds then. They don't take up any room in a carpetbag at all."

"Fine, you'll find seeing the consul interesting," said Miss Doramae. At that moment Ophelia handed me a cup of tea.

We ladies didn't talk about Mr. Ulrich at all, but about the bicycle-built-for-two. Doramae said that she hoped to see Maud very soon.

"I know that she wants to get to know you better," I told her. "But I hope you'll make a friend of Miss Belle Cantrell, the lady who sold you some lace at the Emporium."

Doramae smiled. "I intend to. I liked her right away. She'll be coming to call today, too."

175

"That's good. My brother Elbert likes her, and she likes him. Even if he's younger than Michael, Elbert's getting on and should be getting married, too."

"*Lacy!*" Ophelia whispered to me, shaking her head, so I shut up. But I got the words out!

Just then the men came back. How Pa was grinning! "Time to go home, Lacy," he said. "We have to let the other visitors have some room to sit down in. This house ain't big enough to hold a lot of company at one time."

I put down my teacup, then looked at Michael, who was smiling at Pa. "Remember, Pa, let Lacy have the final say on what I asked you to do."

"What's that?" I wanted to know.

"Pa will tell you on the way home, Lacy. Give my best to old Elbert." Michael lifted me off the floor in a rib-cracking hug and muttered into my ear, "Thanks, Lacy. You know what I mean."

"Don't bite the dentist the way you did a few years back," Hector said, as we left.

Once Pa and I were on El Dorado Street, I asked, "What am I supposed to have the final say on?"

He chuckled, hauled a tiny piece of string out of the watch pocket of his vest, and dangled it in front of my eyes.

"What's that, Pa?"

"The size of her finger. Mike gave it to me out in the kitchen."

I stopped walking. "Doramae's finger?"

"That's right. Mike asked us to buy a ring in Frisco.

He wants one with a pearl in it, because she likes pearls. He couldn't find one like that here in town."

"Oh, Pa, does she know about it?"

"How else would he be able to get the string around her finger?"

By golly, Michael had courted her faster than Hector. He was giving her an engagement ring already.

Pa went on. "Mike says that Doramae wants you to pick it out because you're a lady. Hector told us where to stay in Frisco and where to buy the ring. The place will give us quality at a fair price even if we're out-of-town folks."

I didn't say another word all the way home. Apparently I would have plenty to do in Frisco besides seeing the dentist. In addition to the tooth and the pearl ring and the British consul, there was Elbert, too.

The thought had come to my mind that if Elbert married Belle Cantrell, there'd be a redheaded Mrs. Bingham as well as a blond and a brunette one. And they'd be the three prettiest ladies on Coyote Mountain, for sure!

I had to remember to hook the yellow sunbonnet over the tree limb to tell Maud the news. It would hearten her plenty to know that we were being successful at last.

On the train that was taking us to Frisco my tooth didn't twinge once until dinner time. Pa told me when I let out a small howl in the dining car, "You ought to know better than to pile cold ice cream on top of a bad tooth. Well, what do you think of train travel anyhow, Lacy?"

"It's wonderful," I said. That night, when I climbed into the upper bunk of the sleeping car, I thought some more about what made train travel so good. It was thrilling to watch the countryside disappear while you looked out a train window. Going from the Pullman car to the dining car was an adventure because the train swayed so, and the doors between the cars were so heavy it took all of a girl's strength to pull one open. The food in the dining car was something very special—roast beef, corn on the cob, oyster soup, mashed potatoes and gravy, and even peach ice cream. Watching the Pullman seats turned almost magically into upper and lower berths was one of the most wondrous things I'd ever seen. I liked the porters and the conductor and dining-car waiters, everything, everybody!

Our train came to the end of its journey sometime during the night, settling down on solid ground at the east end of San Francisco Bay. Pa had warned me that we'd have to go over the water to Frisco on a special kind of boat called a "ferryboat."

He and I got out of our sleeping car in the morning, and then I had my first sight of something other than mountains, canyons, mesas, and creeks. How enormous the Bay was and how blue the water in the sunshine! I could hardly believe that the Pacific Ocean would be bigger, but I knew from my geography books back home that it surely was.

## "Get It Done Down There"

Along with Pa, I went down to the ferry landing and waited, watching the broad, white-painted boat coming over the Bay. Riding on it was most thrilling, too. I had never been on a boat before, and I stood on the deck with Pa, letting the Bay breeze blow my hair. We watched sea gulls in the white water behind the ferry and sniffed strange scents. Some of them were salt-smelling, some fishy, and some just plain awful. A boy my age standing at the rail next to me said, "Them's mud flats you smell. Pretty."

I turned to say something to him but didn't when I saw the big tin button on his coat lapel. He was full of brass. It said, "If You Like Me, Honey, Grin."

San Francisco appeared to be mostly white, yellow, and gray buildings, and lots of it seemed to have been built on hills. The city was just full of hills with houses on them. Down near the Bay a lot of brown and gray buildings were so tall they made you catch your breath. Some of them were at least four stories up into the air.

The Bay was filled with big sailing ships and steamboats like ours. They were whistling and tooting at one another, and wherever I looked I saw a forest of masts.

Our ferry came into a low, brown shed that wasn't one bit elegant, even if it was the Ferry Building. We got off the boat and walked across a square paved with planks. The square was full of men and boys yelling at the top of their lungs, trying to grab our carpetbags out of Pa's hands.

"What are they yelling?" I cried to Pa, who was holding tight to our bags. Now and then he kicked out at somebody who was grabbing at them without his permission.

"The names of hotels, Lacy," he shouted back. "They'll send us in a hotel buggy to where we want to go. Hector warned me about these here galoots. Listen hard for the name of the Palace Hotel."

I did listen hard, and when I heard a thin, bearded man yelling, "Palace, Palace!" I grabbed Pa by the coattail and pointed. The man from the Palace Hotel, the place Hector suggested, got hold of our bags in a flash and started off at a run for a waiting line of buggies. We followed him and got into the buggy where he had set the bags. After Pa had thrown the hotel runner a ten-cent piece, the driver of the rig started up without a word to us, and off we went at a fast trot into the city of San Francisco.

In all my life I'd never seen so many people, wagons, buggies, and carriages, and they all were moving. Men and ladies walked fast; horses trotted, or if they were pulling heavy wagonloads, they walked fast, too. Every inch of the broad street called Market Street was filled with buildings set right up against each other with no spaces in between.

The chestnut horse that pulled our rig had nerves of iron, it seemed to me, because he never once shied. And when we turned off Market Street and a big red-and-yellow, box-shaped metal machine came clanging directly toward him, he only twitched his ears. The

thing sailed clattering past us while I clutched at Pa
and the driver of our rig laughed.

"It's all right, Lacy. The horses here are used to it;
so will we be after a while. I read about these things
in the paper. They're electric trolleys. They call 'em
cable cars because they run on steel cables set down
in the street. We ought to take a ride on one of 'em
before we go."

I let go of Pa and stared after the cable car. People
weren't only inside the open-air contraption, they
were hanging along the wooden steps that ran the
length of it on each side. I was still marveling at such
recklessness when our rig turned back onto Market
Street, where the trolleys were horse-drawn and
looked more natural.

Oh, I had lots to marvel at that first day in Frisco!
First of all, there was the Palace Hotel. It was mag-
nificent, seven stories tall. Our rig drove right up inside it, where we were met by men in beautiful frock
coats. From the carriage entrance we went into an
enormous room that was all marble floors, golden-oak
furniture, plush-and-velvet chairs, and dozens of
gleaming brass spittoons.

Pa got sparkling clean rooms for us on the second
floor. I looked mine over and then Pa's. Both of them
had tables and bureaus and gaslights and gold-rimmed
mirrors and a big bed. His had red draperies and a red
carpet, and mine was deep blue. The marble top of my
bureau was veined with pink and his with black.

I was too impressed with what I was seeing to feel

my tooth aching. But Pa reminded me of it when he said, "We better go downstairs now, Lacy, and see about gettin' in touch with that dentist galoot on Mission Street."

I sighed. "How will we get there, Pa?"

"I dunno. We'll ask at the hotel desk and see what they have to suggest."

What they said astonished me. They told Pa to use the telephone instrument to call the dentist's office. The clerk showed Pa what to do. I listened to the cranking, then the voice of the lady operator, and then another lady in Dr. Friend's office. She made the appointment for the next morning at ten o'clock.

Clear as could be, I heard the voice tell Pa, "Don't let the child eat any breakfast, Mr. Bingham."

I wasn't pleased, but didn't complain. "Maybe there's a telephone at the boardinghouse where Elbert lives. Then you could telephone there and ask somebody to give him a message to come down here and eat supper with us. The lady didn't say that I couldn't have any supper."

"I'll see about that right now, Lacy." Pa found out from the hotel clerk that Mrs. Wilkinson's boardinghouse on Steiner Street had a telephone, so he called and talked with her. I listened and heard every word. First she told Pa not to yell. She said Elbert was just fine, and she'd give him the message when he came in from work.

I called the lace shop in North Beach next and said thank-you to Madame Thérèse. I could barely understand what she was saying because of her queer French accent, but I did get that she was pleased to have been able to help me. She said, too, that she was still very sure the lacework was Irish.

"I think that the telephone is a dandy invention," I told Pa. "Better than the telegraph any day. We ought to put one in the house and livery stable just as soon as Coyote Mountain gets telephones."

"It could lead to laziness," he said, as we sat down in the lobby. "All talking and less and less walking. Well, I'll think about it when the time comes."

"I wonder if Elbert has changed? There are so many unusual things here, he might have, Pa."

Pa laughed. "Elbert? Not him. Maybe he's changed his shirt a couple of times since he's been here, but I bet that's about all. He ain't a man to be affected by where he is, though all this newfangled machinery ought to have held his interest."

Elbert hadn't changed much. He was his old self, as shaggy as ever, but he had put on his brown-striped suit and a bowler hat. He hugged me and shook Pa's hand over and over. Before we went into the café Elbert took us out into a courtyard filled with bushy green trees he called "palms." He pointed to the ceiling and said, "Wait here a minute, both of you, and you'll see something to remember all your lives."

We looked up and in a few minutes saw a whole bunch of lights suddenly wink on all by themselves.

"What are they?" I asked Elbert.

"Are they some new kind of gaslight, son?"

"Nope, they ain't gaslights at all. They're electric lights, Mr. Thomas Edison's invention. They're the coming thing in this country."

Pa smiled. "Well, they are sort of spectacular, I guess. Have you come up with anything spectacular yourself?"

"Not yet, but I'm keepin' busy down at the foundry workin' for my boss. I like him a lot, Pa."

"I want to come visit you down there after Lacy sees the dentist tomorrow."

"Sorry, Pa. You can't do that. The boss won't let anybody but his workers inside. His motto is: No Visitors."

"All right, Elbert. You come here to see us. You can show us the town later on. Now Lacy and me are tired. We been walking up and down the streets all day, and we need a good supper. Sight-seeing is hard work."

As we went out of the Palm Court, Elbert asked me, "How's your tooth, Lacy?"

"It hurts a little bit now and then." I came closer to him. "Elbert, we'll tell you at supper about Michael's getting engaged to a lady fiddle player who can walk on ceilings and on a tightrope, too. But before we do, I want to say that Belle Cantrell is still single, and I know for a fact she still likes you best of all the Bingham brothers."

He cleared his throat. "Well, now. Do tell, Lacy, do tell. Where did Mike find such a lady? Is he happy?"

"Oh, yes, Elbert, he sure is."

Pa chimed in. "Leastwise, being engaged to little

184

Doramae sure agrees with him. Lacy and me will tell you all about how he got to know her. A lot has happened since you've been gone, and Lacy can bring you up-to-date."

I only smiled and nodded. If I told the two of them about Miss Veronica Eccles Vernon the hair on their heads would stand straight on end. I hadn't mentioned anything to Pa about the British consul either, for fear he'd say I shouldn't pester such an important man. But I did plan to pester him. This trip seemed to be my only chance.

## ≥ 11

# Dr. Friend and the
# Honorable Mr. Littleton-Jones

I needed every bit of my courage to get into the horse
cab that was to take us to the dentist's office the next
morning. Now I could see why the lady had said I
wasn't to eat any breakfast. If I'd had any, it would
have turned to rock by the time our cab turned off
Market Street onto Seventh and then onto Mission,
which was almost as busy as Market.

My tooth had ached off and on through the night,
so I hadn't slept too well in my elegant brass bed. Also,
I heard all the other hotel guests walking up and down
the hallway all night long.

Pa had given the driver the dentist's address, and
we pulled up at a brick building. He led me inside and

up a flight of steps. At the head of the stairs was an elegant black-and-gold sign with a big gold tooth hanging from a gold chain. The sign read:

Dr. R.L. Friend, Dentist
A True Blue Friend to All Who Suffer
A Painless Practitioner
Hours: 8 A.M. TO 6 P.M., Monday to Saturday

Pa opened the carved-oak door and pushed me into the dentist's waiting room. It wasn't like Dr. Cantrell's. It was as elegant as the Palace Hotel, with purple-velvet portieres and red-plush settees and chairs. There wasn't a stuffed animal in sight, though there were some folks sitting around holding their faces.

All at once there came a sound, one I'd never heard in Dr. Cantrell's office, a happy squealing, then somebody laughing.

A door opened and a pretty fair-haired lady in a long pink-and-white-striped apron over a gray dress came out. She had a white card in her hand.

"Miss Bingham?" she called out.

I got up. "That's me, ma'am."

She smiled at me. "Come along. Dr. Friend will take you next."

*Next!* That terrible word. Pa grunted at me, and somehow I moved my legs across to the door and into a little room where there was the same sort of metal chair that Dr. Cantrell had at home. I climbed up into it and had a towel put over my chest.

A door opened to the side, and in bounced a dark-haired man wearing spectacles, a bright-red cravat with a diamond stickpin, and a white coat that hung to the tops of his shoes.

He nodded to the pretty lady, and then he smiled at me. "Open up, little lady." I did, and he gazed and gazed into my mouth. "Shut it, please."

Once more he nodded to the lady. I heard the whirring sound of wheels coming up behind me, and out of the corner of one eye I saw some big cigar-shaped things on a metal cart. The things had rubber tubes hanging out of their top and little wheels alongside the hoses.

"All right, Barbara," the dentist said to the lady behind me.

All at once, something came crackling down over my head. I had a glimpse of a brown-paper bag. Then I heard a hissing sound, and I felt the rubber tubes, one on each side of my face. I smelled something queer for an instant and heard the dentist saying, "Grab her around the neck, Barbara. Keep the gas and oxygen up in there till I tell you to let her go."

While I thrashed my limbs around, I felt the lady clasping the bag around my neck. She was strong as well as pretty.

Suddenly I forgot about her and about the bag. I was floating away on a big white ferryboat on San Francisco Bay while Maud, who stood beside me and tickled me, told me some good jokes. They made me laugh, so I tickled her, and she laughed until all at once I knew where I was. I could see Dr. Friend in front of me, smiling and holding my bad tooth in a pair of pliers.

"It's all over, and I bet you didn't feel a thing after we gave you whiffs of laughing gas."

"No, sir, I didn't." Still feeling giggly, I put my hand to my neck and said, "The whiffs were just fine, but I did feel something when the lady tried to choke me."

"I was simply trying to keep the gas up in the bag. It's the very latest method of giving anesthesia." She sounded slightly annoyed.

Dr. Friend added, "Yes, indeedy. Once upon a time all I could have done for you, little lady, would be to give you lots of whiskey or a tap on the head with a wooden mallet."

I shakily got out of the chair. "I guess this is better than those things. What do I do now?"

"Enjoy San Francisco. I hear tell you're from out of town. Well, you'll be here another four days to see how your mouth and jaw feel. If you have trouble, ring me on the telephone and come back here. Now go out through that door over there, not through my waiting room. Your papa will meet you outside. Good-bye, little lady."

I thanked the dentist and went outside. Sure enough, Pa was there to help me down the steps to the street. "It couldn't have been too bad," he said. "I heard you laughing in there."

"That was the laughing gas you heard, not really me. It didn't hurt one bit, though. Dr. Cantrell was right about that, but he was wrong as could be about the other thing."

"What was that, honey?"

"The floor of his room wasn't paved with teeth he'd pulled. It was plain wood with a purple-and-gold carpet on it."

Pa laughed, then asked, "Did he give you your tooth as a souvenir?"

"No, he didn't even offer it to me, and if he did, I don't know what I would have done with it back home." I paused for a moment. "Pa, I know I'll be all right soon, but I think I'd like to rest up in my room this afternoon. Maybe if I don't feel up to snuff, I might stay there tomorrow, too. Why don't you look at the livery stables here in Frisco tomorrow and go wherever Hector goes to buy horses for us?"

"I don't think it would be right to leave you alone, Lacy."

"Well, you might stay with me this afternoon, but you go on out tomorrow! Don't worry about me. The hole in my head where that tooth used to be doesn't hurt me much now, so it probably won't tomorrow. You might as well mosey about and see as much of the city as you can. I'll be just fine in my room, looking out the window."

I was trying my best to get him to go out by himself, so I could have the day to do the things I wanted. No, he'd never let me go to the British consul by myself, and I was very sure he wouldn't go there with me.

Finally, he said, "All right, Lacy, I'll mosey about a

bit tomorrow. Yep, I do know where Hector got those black geldings that pull the hearse. I'll go make the acquaintance of the gents there. Come on now, let's hail a horse cab and get you back to the hotel."

Pa and I had a very elegant breakfast of oyster omelet and grilled ham the next morning, and right afterward he went off to visit places where Hector had done horse and harness business. I was sure he'd be gone most of the day, because he'd also want to visit some of Frisco's saloons, just to compare them with the ones we had in Coyote Mountain.

A little later I went out, too, feeling fine in spite of a sore jaw. I folded up my baby duds and took them with me in the purse dangling from my wrist. The purse had a lot of nickels in it, too. I'd learned they were the fare on the horsecars and cable cars, and I planned to do some traveling.

Although I was dressed in my best straw hat and gloves and navy-blue sailor-collar outfit, I was worried that horse-cars wouldn't stop for a child. I wished that I was already wearing the long skirts Ophelia was sewing for me. Still, a horsecar stopped when I waited in the right place near Lotta's Fountain, and the nice driver told me the number of the car I needed to get to Battery Street. That was where the British consul was located, down by the wharves.

The right-numbered horse trolley came along finally. I rode through tall buildings until the driver halted his horse, called out, "Battery Street!" and pointed to the place I wanted, number 506. It was a narrow, brick house with an iron fence in front. On the wall was a red shield with a little golden crown. Simple black letters spelled *British Consulate.*

Underneath was: *British Consul General, The Honorable Mr. Edward Littleton-Jones*

There wasn't one word there about Queen Victoria, who was his boss, but Mr. Littleton-Jones was the one I wanted, all right. So I got off the horsecar, thanking the driver politely, and went up the steps of 506. I knew what I wanted to say, and I had my baby duds with me, but as I opened the door I wondered if an appointment was necessary. I hadn't called up on the telephone first the way Frisco folks did. Had I done a bad thing? Were honorable consuls fussy about such matters?

There was a desk in the front hall, and behind it sat a redheaded young gentleman dressed in a dark-blue frock coat. I asked, "Are you the honorable consul general, mister?"

He smiled and shook his head. In a high-pitched voice he said, "No, I am employed here, however. Perhaps I can help you? You aren't British, are you? Or are you Canadian perhaps?"

"Oh, no," I told him. "I'm not any of those things. I may be Irish, but I'm not sure. Maybe the Irish I am is American—or it was American."

"You seem to be quite confused about matters, miss."

"You bet I am. Please, let me tell you the story."

So I told him how I came to the Binghams. He listened carefully and politely, then nodded. "Yes, I do believe the consul would like to talk to you, miss. I'll tell him you're here."

I said, "I hope it won't take long to see him. I can't stay here all day."

"Oh, that won't be necessary. He'll be free in a couple of minutes, I'm sure. He's attending to some paper work now."

"Do you suppose he could tell me something about the Irish people here in California in 1880?" I asked.

"I don't know, but you did come to the proper place to begin with." The young man got up, went down the little hall, rapped on a door, and went inside.

A little while later a tall, gray-coated, elderly man with a big, white, bristling mustache came out. He looked at me and I looked at him. He surely looked honorable to me, and kindly, to boot.

The young one joined him and beckoned to me. I walked down the hall to both of them and into a red-and-gold wallpapered room with a bay window and deep red-velvet draperies.

"Please sit down, miss," said the young man, and left the room.

The white-haired gentleman sat behind a desk and said in a very gentle, deep, slow voice, "I hear that you have a story to tell me, that you may or may not be Irish?"

"Yes, sir. Maybe I am." I wasn't scared of him at all.

"Start at the beginning, please, and tell me why you think so."

193

"Yes, sir." I hauled out the baby duds and set them on his desk. I told him about being left on the veranda, the silent watchdogs and the Indian things, and finally about what the Frisco lace lady, Madame Thérèse, had written.

"And you appeared on this veranda at a place later called Coyote Mountain in the year 1880?" he asked.

"Yes, sir, in April, 1880. I was born in 1879, though, because I was a couple of months old then. Or at least Ma Bingham thought so."

He put his long fingers together to make a steeple. "I came over here from England as consul in 1882, so that was before my time, but I do recall having heard something remarkable from the staff here about Irish settlers. They came from the north of Ireland, from County Antrim, and they settled in a small valley called Beaver Meadows, wherever that may be. I believe it was supposed to be in Yolo County."

"Yolo County? That's two counties west of us in Coyote Mountain."

"Is it now?" He nodded at me. "There were four families, men, women, and children, who filed on that land and built their homes, planning eventually to become American citizens."

I thought there was a strange look on his face. "Didn't they?" I asked.

"No, they didn't." He shook his head. "They were killed, you see—murdered. Massacred would be the right word, I fear."

"Indians?" I breathed.

194

"No, not Indians. Outlaws. I was told that white criminals robbed, then shot the Irish settlers."

Murdered? I picked up my baby duds and, trembling, stuffed them into my purse. "Were there any babies?"

"There may well have been infants among the four families."

I sighed. "Well, maybe I was one of their babies, and that's why I had the Irish-lace things on me."

"Perhaps, though I have no idea. If you want to pursue the matter, why don't you go to the San Francisco public library and ask to see old copies of the state's newspapers? They would surely have carried that horrible story. Libraries keep files of newspapers, you know."

"No, I didn't know. Thank you." I got up, and then I curtseyed because he was the sort of old gent one did that to. "You've been very good to me when I don't even know if I'm Irish or not, and you didn't have to help me."

"I found it a pleasure. I wish that I had been able to give you happier facts, though." He got up, too, and sort of bowed to me. Then he sat down again and looked at the pile of papers in front of him.

At the outside desk I asked the young man where the Frisco library was.

"Inside the city hall."

"Thank you. You've both sure been honorable to me here. Are all consuls so honorable as the old gent? He's sure a brick."

He chuckled. "Not quite so honorable as Mr. Littleton-Jones. You see, consuls are given the courtesy title of Honorable whoever they happen to be, but as the brother of an earl in England Mr. Littleton-Jones is called Honorable even if he is not in the consular service but only a private gentleman-farmer in England."

"You mean he's the Honorable Honorable Mr. Littleton-Jones?"

"Exactly!"

"My!" The British were certainly a remarkable kind of people. I curtseyed to the young man, too, and went to wait for the next horse trolley coming up Battery Street.

While I waited, I thought about what I'd just learned. There had been Irish folks living not too far from Coyote Mountain, although they were dead Irishmen. I sure couldn't go to Yolo County and ask these Irishmen about myself, could I? Those poor killed settlers more than likely didn't mean anything in my life, but what I'd heard about them was surely interesting. Yep, I would go to the library. It wasn't even noontime yet, and my jaw wasn't giving me any trouble. Tomorrow I'd have to help Pa get the ring for Doramae, and afterward Elbert had promised to show us the city. If I was going to get to the library, today was the only time to do so.

When the horse trolley showed up, I boarded and asked the driver how to get to the San Francisco city hall, which turned out to be not too far from the Palace Hotel.

The public library was in the part of the city hall that had the smaller of two domes on top. I went up some steps until I came to a desk in a very big room filled with books. Because the desk was right in front of the door I'd come through, I went up to it and stood waiting for the clerk to look up from the work he was doing, putting some white cards into a wooden box.

He smiled. "Yes, little lady, what can I do for you?"

He seemed sensible, so I came right to the point. "I need to see newspapers from this state—old ones—but I don't really know exactly when, mister. I want to find out about some people, four families from Ireland, who settled in Yolo County back in the late 1870's. What I want to know about happened sometime between January and April of 1880, I think. That was when they all got murdered. Would that kind of news be in papers here in San Francisco, news from Yolo County, I mean?"

"Murders of entire families? Oh, yes, indeed. The news would surely be on the very first pages."

"That's good to hear. I haven't got all day."

"Please come with me." He led the way to a very long table in an even bigger room. There he went up to a counter to speak to a lady with a piled-up pompadour and jet necklace. She nodded and left.

I sat down to wait, and soon she was back with the

biggest book I'd ever seen. She slid it down in front of me and said, "This is the *Alta California* for the month of January, 1880. All of that month's issues are bound together here. The library page will bring you February, and when you need March and April, come to the counter and tell me."

"Yes, ma'am. Thank you."

I started in on January, looking quickly up and down the front page of each day. By the time I was at January 15, a page brought me the whole month of February. Because it was the shortest month, it went faster, even though 1880 was a leap year.

I went back to the counter. "I guess I need March and April now, please."

The lady rang a bell, and the same page came out of a door. "The next two months are also required," she said.

Well, he brought them all at once. He was mighty muscular, I thought, as he lugged both January and February off, puffing a bit.

I found what I was looking for in the upper left-hand column of the front page of March 31. The heading said:

*Recent Irish Settlers Slain at Beaver Meadows*

The article was so horrible it made my scalp prickle. Unknown killers had attacked four farms, shot the people dead, then burned their houses and barns. It was believed that the motive for the murders was robbery and that the killings were the work of the notorious Thompson gang. In all, some nineteen settlers who had emigrated in 1878 from County Antrim to Yolo County were thought to have been killed and their bodies burned in the fires the killers had set. The last names of the Irish families were given: O'Toole, Murphy, Ahearne, and De Lacy.

I sat for a long time, clutching at my purse. Was one of those families my real family? Well, if so, I hadn't found out from this newspaper article.

I was reading the article for the third time when a shadow fell over the page. I looked up to see the librarian, who asked me, "Did you find what you were looking for?"

I sighed and whispered, "In a way I did, I think. But I don't know where to go from here. I guess there isn't anywhere to go." Then I had an idea. "Were you here in this state in 1880, mister?"

"Yes, I was."

I pointed to the newspaper article. "Would you remember reading about this?"

He read over my shoulder. "The Thompson gang? Oh, yes, I remember them. The Thompson gang got their comeuppance in 1880, April of that year, as I recall. I remember it happened about the same time I got married."

"What day did you get married?"

"April 28." He smiled and went back to the counter and the jet-necklace lady.

I struggled now with April, reading from the

twenty-fifth through to the twenty-ninth. On the thirtieth I found what I'd been looking for, all right! This heading said:

*Outlaw Gang Killed in Mountain Pass. Six Dead.*

This article was longer than the other one, but still just one column. The Thompson gang, which seemed to be mostly Thompson brothers, had attacked a train in a pass in the Sierras, hoping to get a shipment of gold bullion. The bullion was guarded on that trip by soldiers, but the Thompsons didn't know it. The soldiers, who were crack shots, defended the train. They shot and killed all the outlaws, except for one man, a Paiute Indian. He died of wounds a little after the others. Before he died, he talked to the captain of the troopers and told him about the gang's attack on some settlers in Yolo County and the burning of their houses the month before. The names of the gang members were listed: four Thompsons, a Bailey, and the Indian, who was known only as Paiute Dick.

Dick? Paiute Dick?

*Little Dick?*

## ❧ 12

# Something Spectacular!

I went to the counter. "Please, can I leave March and April here on the table till I can get my pa to come here and read them, too? It's very important to me. Will you be staying open till five o'clock?"

"Yes, we will. We'll hold the volumes behind the counter for you until that time," the lady assured me.

I found Pa back at the hotel. He was sitting on the edge of his bathtub, his feet soaking in cold water. I supposed he'd done a lot of walking around.

"Well, did you finally get up? The beds are good here, all right. I came back over an hour ago. How's your jaw? I didn't knock on your door when I came in, because I thought you might still be sleeping."

"I wasn't. Pa, please put on your socks and shoes and come down to city hall with me. There's something I want to show you."

He laughed. "I don't want to meet the mayor! My feet are on fire from all these danged cement sidewalks here. Give me a boardwalk any day."

"It isn't to meet the mayor. I'm not joking, and I didn't sleep at all today. I've been out all day long same as you. I'm sorry, but I just had to go out. I had errands to do here in Frisco."

As he reached for a towel at the end of his bed, he said, "I suppose you went to that jewelry store to look at Doramae's ring, huh? You already picked it out for style?"

"No, Pa. We're going to do that tomorrow, remember? Pa, have you ever heard of some outlaws called the Thompson gang?"

He put on a sock. "Yep, but that was a long time back. They're all dead, as I recall, all killed by the United States Army."

"That's right, they were." While he put on his other sock and his shoes, I told him about the Honorable Honorable Mr. Littleton-Jones and the library and the articles in the March and April, 1880, newspapers. I included everything but the Paiute Indian with the gang.

"Well, well," he commented. "Maybe those Irish families were your real folks, Lacy. All right, let's go to the library, and I'll read them papers, too."

We went by horse cab to the city hall and walked

to the counter where the lady stood. The page brought March and April back to the table, and I opened both to the right pages so Pa could read the articles.

He read them, then sat back for a moment with his hand to his forehead. I'd seen how his finger had paused over the name of the Indian, just as mine had.

I asked in a whisper, "Well, Pa?"

"Maybe so, Lacy. Maybe so," he replied softly.

We walked back to the Palace Hotel together. For a time Pa was silent. Then he said, "You know, that Paiute Indian could have been our Little Dick. He could have brought you to Ma and left you on the veranda in a basket and blanket he'd got from his own tribe. If he got killed with the Thompsons, he must have ridden with them, and he would have been in on the killing of the Irishmen. That would mean he'd changed a lot from the time Ma and I knew him. Dick might very well have fetched you to Ma. He used to bring her pretty rocks and bird feathers and such things. It wouldn't surprise me one bit if he knew she hankered after a baby girl, and when one crossed his path, he thought of her and went out of his way to get it to her." Pa shook his head. "The dogs sure liked that Indian boy. That would explain their not barking that night you showed up on the veranda. And even if the Thompsons knew he planned to bring a settler's baby to Ma, they wouldn't have had any cause to stop him. It wasn't as if you, a baby, could tell a sheriff what they'd done."

"Maybe you're right, Pa. I dunno." I felt down-in-the-mouth because the story of the Irish folks and Pa's Indian friend was very sad. Maybe this Paiute wasn't Little Dick, but Little Dick had never come back to the Binghams either.

"Lacy," Pa asked me, as we passed a tobacco shop, "who do you want to think you are—Lacy Murphy, Lacy O'Toole, Lacy Ahearne, or Lacy de Lacy? You've got four choices."

"I'm Lacy Bingham, Pa. That's who I'll always be." I sighed. "But you know, I do think one of them is my true family. I think my real mother or grandma made the lace bonnet and trimmed the gown back in Ireland. I bet I wasn't the first baby in that family to wear those duds either. A lot of work went into them."

"And a lot of love, too," agreed Pa. "I have the feeling that those Irish folks were good people. They would have made fine United States citizens, the kind to be proud of."

"Thank you for saying that, Pa. Thank you for everything."

We had supper alone that night in the hotel and went to bed early. When I said my prayers, I put in some more folks to be blessed besides just Binghams and Rowbottoms. I added the names of the Irish families and of Little Dick, and then I fell asleep.

Pa and I went to Colonel Andrew's Diamond Palace

the next morning and got a gold ring with a nice creamy pink pearl for Doramae. It was easy to agree on because it was the prettiest one in the tray.

The rest of that day we spent with Elbert, who'd taken two days off from his mysterious work at the foundry. We were at the Cliff House at the ocean's edge, watching the seals on the rocks below, when I told him about the Irish folks and the outlaws and the Indian with them.

"I remember Dick," Elbert said. "That would be the sort of thing he'd do, too, if he thought it'd tickle Ma. And if Dick was with outlaws, then he wouldn't have hung around our stagecoach station because he wouldn't want them to get the idea to rob us."

"That's what came through my mind, too," said Pa. "Well, let's see Frisco now and not talk about outlaws anymore. Let's have some good times while we're here."

The three of us saw everything from Chinatown to the Presidio at the Golden Gate Park—where the Bay meets the Pacific Ocean—to old Mission Dolores, the first church in Frisco.

On our very last night, we all went to the Tivoli Opera House to see a play. How proud I was to sit between Pa and Elbert. I felt nearly as elegant in my blue-batiste dress, even though it was short, as the Frisco ladies looked in their jewels and embroidered satin gowns, which showed off their bare shoulders. Some of the ladies were mighty pretty. I saw how they glanced over their shoulders at Elbert, but he never once glanced back at them. Belle Cantrell would be interested to hear that, for sure.

Back at the Palace Hotel, Pa and I said good-bye to Elbert, who had to go to work in the morning.

"Well, Elbert, ain't you going to breathe a single hint to us about what you've been up to in that foundry?" Pa asked.

"Nope, Pa. I swore to my boss to keep it a secret."

Pa laughed. "What is it? Some kind of secret weapon?"

Elbert wouldn't say. All he did was shake his head and grin, which told us nothing.

The next morning we crossed the Bay to board the eastbound train in Oakland. And again I had another thrilling night aboard a train, sleeping in a berth and eating dining-car food.

The first person I went to see when we got to Coyote Mountain was Maud. I told her about the Frisco dentist and what I'd learned about who I really might be. Oh, but she was excited, but sad, too.

"I think you must truly be Lacy de Lacy, because the last name fits the first name so well."

"Well, I fancy Ahearne, you know, but I don't think my real folks named me Lacy. And I'm very sure now that I wasn't ever a princess."

"How's Elbert?" she asked.

"Busy at his work and danged mysterious about it, too!"

"Is he?" Maud paused. "Well, even if I stayed home, I've got some news for you, too. I read the newspaper here all the time. Your brother Michael is going to get married to Miss Hollister late in the month of September."

"That's good. Pa and I bought the engagement ring down in Frisco. I'd hate to think it was just going to lie around in its box for months and months while they played the fiddle and courted. I'm glad they nailed down the date. Please pardon me now, Maud. I have to go talk to Belle Cantrell."

"Sure, Lacy, I bet you have something interesting to tell her!"

"Oh, Maud, I wish that I did—about Elbert, I mean."

Belle had brought a sandwich for lunch, and while she ate it in the Emporium's storeroom, I sat on a pickle barrel and told her what I'd found out at the San Francisco public library and about my interview with the British consul.

"The consul?" Belle nodded. "That was smart to go see him."

"Doramae Hollister lived down in Frisco, and she was the one who told me about him."

"Of course." Belle grinned at me over her sandwich. "She's marrying your middle brother Michael in a couple of months' time."

"That's right. Golly, would you ever have believed that he could court a lady so fast?"

Belle sighed. "No, as a matter of fact, I wouldn't, but then life is full of surprises. Doramae has asked me to be a bridesmaid for her. I like her very much, and I'm delighted she and Michael are so happy." All at once she changed the subject. "Did you ever really expect to find out who you truly are, as you seem to have done?"

"No, I'd hoped, but I didn't truly expect to. It seems I'm Irish, all right. I guess that I'll go along with what the baby duds say."

She nodded, then said, "But if your parents, whoever they were, had lived, you wouldn't be Irish anymore. You'd be American because they would be by now."

"I suppose so. I never thought of that." I said carefully, "Pa and I saw a lot of Elbert down in Frisco after I went to the dentist."

"How is he?"

"The dentist? You'll have to tell your pa for me that fellow knows his oats." I hitched the almost-empty pickle barrel closer to her chair. "Elbert still likes you. I know he does. I can tell. He and Pa and I went to the theater where a lot of ladies were showing their shoulders bare as peeled eggs, and Elbert didn't give one of them a second glance."

"My," she said calmly. "What is Elbert doing these days?"

"We don't know, Pa and I. He wouldn't tell us. He

said it was secret and hinted it might be sort of special
—or at least his boss thinks it is. Pa asked if it was a
secret weapon, because Elbert's working in a foundry,
but he only shook his head."

"Good Lord, I hope it's not a cannon. I think there
are already too many weapons in the world," said
Belle.

I was horrified. "Elbert would never work on a cannon. He doesn't fancy guns much."

"Is he happy, Lacy?"

"I don't know, Miss Cantrell, but I don't think he's
as happy as Hector and Michael. Do you want me to
let you know when we hear from him again?"

"If you'd like to come tell me, I'd like to know how
he's doing."

"Good!" I leaned forward. "I told him you still fa-
vored him." I got up quickly and left the storeroom
before she could get mad. Oh, she had no idea of
what I'd dared to make my brothers happy men. I'd
never tell anybody in my family about Miss Veronica
Eccles Vernon as long as I lived! A person went
through a lot to make a match!

Weeks went by; I kept house for Pa, put my hair on
top of my head so it would stay there, and started
wearing shirtwaists and the long skirts Ophelia had
made for me. I practiced walking in high heels, too.
Maud, who wobbled about with me, agreed that they
weren't comfortable, but we both knew our days as
eighth-grade girls were gone forever.

Four days before it was time for us to start riding in the mud wagon to the high school in Osborne Valley something happened that made me gasp.

I got a telegram! My very first one. It came up the hill by Western Union messenger. It was from Elbert, and it said that he would be coming through Coyote Mountain on the train day after tomorrow on his way to Denver for his boss. He would stay overnight with us. He also said that he didn't want anybody but Pa and me to meet him at the train depot. It was a long telegram.

The last sentence stopped me from running down to the livery stable. Instead I showed the telegram secretly to Pa after Michael had gone out to his fiddle lessons with Doramae. "Well," Pa said, "this is something, isn't it?"

"Yes, Pa, but what?"

Elbert's return was even more exciting than the arrival of the bicycle-built-for-two late in July. Maud and I had ridden and ridden it, but finally we decided the rutted, trembling streets of Coyote Mountain weren't made for bicycles of any kind. We'd gotten a bit weary of it, and I'd just about talked Maud into giving it to Doramae and Michael as a wedding present from the two of us. After all, we were both involved up to the hilt in that romance.

I was quivering with excitement the day Elbert was to arrive on the Frisco train. Pa was with me on the platform, excited, too, but trying hard not to show it.

When Elbert got off, I had a hard time recognizing him. He hadn't grown a beard or a mustache, but his get-up was very strange. He was wearing a down-to-the-heels brown-cotton coat, a brown cap with a visor, and a pair of big, black-rimmed goggles over his eyes. We weren't sure who he was until he was right in front of us.

Elbert took off the goggles, grabbed Pa's hand, and hugged me. "You folks wait right here for me while I go down to the flatcar and get 'em to unload. Don't you dare move," he said with a wide grin on his face.

"*Flatcar?*" Pa exclaimed. "What travels on a flatcar? He can't be bringing us any new horses, not on a flat-car."

I said, "I don't know what it is, but he acts happier than I've ever seen him. He seems very proud."

"Yep, Elbert does appear to be mighty pleased with himself today, don't he? I wonder why that would be."

We learned the reason a couple of minutes later. Some men came out of a boxcar carrying planks and walked with them to the rear of the train where the flatcars were. Then one of them returned with a folded canvas tarpaulin under one arm and a rope coiled over his shoulder and went into the boxcar again.

"Whatever Elbert's got back there is all covered up, and it's got to come off on them planks. It's got to be good size, too, because that tarpaulin is big," Pa said.

Suddenly we heard a roaring and popping sound

loud enough to split our eardrums. Then it hove into view, advancing over the platform. Folks leaped out of the way, and passengers aboard the train stared out their windows.

It was a machine! It had four wheels and looked like a black buggy, but it was going along all by itself. Elbert was sitting in it and seemed to be making it go. It came snorting and bucking right up to Pa and me and stopped, shaking and jerking, so close I could have reached out and touched it.

Pa yelled over the clatter, "Elbert, what in the devil is that thing you've got?"

"A buggyaut, Pa! She's got a gas engine, not an electric one, and she can go ten miles an hour on the flat. She steers by a tiller, the rod I'm holdin' onto. Come on, Lacy, hop in for a spin."

Pa got me by the shoulders. "You ain't gettin' in that contraption, Lacy. It might blow sky-high any minute!"

"No, Pa, it won't blow up," Elbert cried.

I kept my eyes on the buggyaut. It seemed to me to want me to get in, it was quivering so. "Please, Pa!" I begged.

"All right then, but you take good care of her, Elbert."

I ran around to the side and got in. Elbert sent the buggyaut on its way along the long board platform and then down off the unloading ramp at its very end. We went out onto Main Street. Over all the noise the buggyaut made, Elbert shouted, "We could've made us a steam or an electric one, but my boss heard that Mr. Thomas Edison told a man named Ford that the gasoline car is the best thing. So that's what my boss and me and the other men made. Ain't it spectacular, though?"

"I think it's the most spectacular thing I ever set eyes on." I yelled back. "Who does it belong to? Is it yours?"

"Nope, it belongs to my boss. He put up the money to build it. I'm still workin' for him. He's sending me out on tour with it now."

We were chugging down Main Street, and were we ever being noticed! Lots of folks had come out of their stores to find out what the racket was, and how they did gape! Others were too busy to do so because they were trying to control their horses. Every horse on Main Street was going crazy—rearing in the traces or running away with the wagon or buggy it was hitched to. Just about every dog in town was chasing us, barking his head off, trying to bite the buggyaut's wheels. It was thrilling!

As we came to El Dorado Street, the hearse went flying past us, with Hector sawing on the reins of the black geldings. Elbert halted the buggyaut out of respect while the carriages following the hearse streaked past us, also at a gallop. The wait gave us time to wave to the mayor, who was gawking from the steps of the town hall, and for Elbert to take off his hat and goggles so he might be recognized by the volunteer firemen in the firehouse. Some of them came dashing up to congratulate him. Oh, he'd showed them all right! He had brought something to town that was spectacular enough to make him noticed.

Then we were off again, snorting our way toward the far end of Main Street. I had a glimpse of Maud, Harvey, and Mrs. Rowbottom, staring popeyed from the doorway of the post office. I waved to them as Elbert skillfully dodged runaway horses by steering a zig-zag path down the street. "It's Elbert. It's a buggy-aut!" I called out to Maud.

Finally we came abreast of the Emporium, and I shouted into Elbert's ear. "Stop here, please."

He stopped by pulling on something somewhere, and I got out. "Wait a minute," I yelled.

He nodded as the machine quivered and jiggled.

I ran up the steps, over the boardwalk, and inside the store where the windows were lined with gaping clerks and customers. I found Belle Cantrell putting a bolt of dark-blue serge back on the shelf.

"It's Elbert," I said. "He's come back with the most spectacular thing Coyote Mountain has ever seen. He doesn't want me really. He's waiting outside for you, Belle." I grabbed her by both hands and dragged her out of the Emporium. "Come on, come on!"

Elbert was sitting in the buggyaut, and when he saw Belle, he did a wonderful thing. He stood up and lifted his hat to her, then put it over his breast for a moment while he bowed. Finally he gestured toward the seat beside him.

I gave her a tiny push. "Go on, Belle."

She gave me a smile, then gathered up her skirts and went down the steps into the street. Taking Elbert's outstretched hand, she stepped into the buggy-aut and sat down beside him.

An instant later he let go of whatever had stopped the machine, grabbed hold of the tiller, and off they went, jerking down Main Street in a cloud of pale-blue smoke. Through the smoke, I saw him put his arm around her shoulders.

I leaned against one of the porch posts and watched them disappear, bucking around the bend at the end of the street and out into the open country. I could hear the buggyaut banging away long after it was out of sight.

A few minutes later Maud came up to me, pushing the tandem, which she kept for us on her back porch. "Shall we follow them, Lacy?" she asked.

"For goodness sake, no! Do you want to ruin everything, Maud Rowbottom? He'll talk to her once he gets that thing stopped somewhere."

"I guess you're right." Maud laughed. "I saw you get out so Belle Cantrell could get in. Did Elbert tell you to, Lacy?"

"No, it was all my own idea."

Maud nodded admiringly. "That was good. I had my doubts about you and me for a while, but both of us, particularly you, turned out to be pretty good match-makers after all. I suppose Elbert'll get married now, too, and then you and your pa will be all alone up there in that big house. In four years you'll graduate out of high school, Lacy, and maybe you'll leave home then, too."

"Maybe so, Maud, but so will you. You won't live with your ma forever."

"That's right, but she'll have Harvey around for a long time yet. By the time that I go she might even like him. He could change, you know. He's already growing out of his listening thing, she says." Maud added, "Your pa won't change, though, and he won't have anybody around the way my ma will. Your pa is too old to change, Lacy. He'll be lonesome." She turned the bicycle around.

I stared at her, annoyed, before I got on the front seat. She asked from behind, "Lacy, have you still got those pink pages out of that magazine I gave you?"

"Sure, they're under my mattress."

"Well, when I looked them over, I saw that there were some widow ladies asking to correspond with gents who were over forty years old. Maybe there's some nice, lonely widow the right age who'd be a good housekeeper and cook."

I swiveled my head to glare at her. "Maud Rowbottom! What are you up to? Start pedaling, please."

As she and I wobbled off in the opposite direction from the one the buggyaut had taken, I thought about what she had said.

Pa? Maybe he was lonesome, and after a while he could get even lonesomer. He looked a bit down-at-the-mouth some nights and claimed he missed Michael sawing away on his fiddle. He'd told me that he missed the sound of his boys' big feet on the steps, too, and that it didn't seem natural not to have doors slamming all the time.

As I steered the bicycle around a big rut I decided to have another look at those rose-pink pages. Come to think about it, Maud was quite right. There might be some lonesome older ladies who would be interested in a handsome widower like Pa, and after all I did have experience in the matter of matchmaking.

# Author's Note

My Coyote Mountain is a composite of several Western mining towns of the early 1890's. My description of shaking streets is based on fact. It wasn't unusual for a mining company to follow a vein of ore under towns and blast away below. The practice was extremely irritating to the nerves of newcomers, who always thought an earthquake was upon them.

I've written here of lovelorn advertisements in magazines of the day. Those ads were a common feature of the late nineteenth century. There are a number of true stories regarding them that make for hilarious reading, but, as can be expected, there were also some unscrupulous adventurers using the ads. Many, of course, were veiled advertisements for products, not for lonesome correspondents at all.

Several magic tricks have appeared in this book, and I've described how they are done. They never failed to enrapture old-time audiences. My source was an 1898 book of stunts and theatrical effects, *Magic, Stage Illusions, and Scientific Diversions, Including Trick Photography*, compiled and edited by Albert A. Hopkins.

When researching turn-of-the-century dentistry, I found myself in much difficulty. Modern dentists are not sure about the paper-bag method of anesthesia, but I know from a pioneer letter that such a homely item was used along with nitrous oxide (laughing gas) and probably oxygen, too. Two dentists suggested how it could have been done. Gases could have been procured in tall metal cylinders with tubing attached. Old photographs of dentists' offices show such equipment.

I've tried to describe the styles, fabrics, and modes of transportation of the early 1890's, as well as use some expressions current then, such as *brick*, a term of esteem.

In an earlier novel for young people, *Blue Stars Watching*, I described 1863 San Francisco. The research I did for that book was of no use in writing this one because in the intervening thirty years the city changed greatly. By 1890 elegant residences had been built on Nob Hill; Chinatown thrived; North Beach became a beach, not part of San Francisco Bay, and splendid hotels and stores were erected. The places I mention by name existed in 1893—the Cliff House,

Lacy Makes a Match

Golden Gate Park, the San Francisco public library in the city hall, Tivoli Opera House, and, of course, the world-famous Palace Hotel. I've tried to depict it as it was, replete with electric lights as well as gaslights. I've written about horse-drawn trolley cars and about that beloved San Francisco institution and trademark, the cable cars. Cable cars flourished in the nineties. A young British journalist by the name of Rudyard Kipling visited the city in 1889, rode on them, and wrote about them. In writing about San Francisco, I've chiefly used *This Was San Francisco* by San Francisco author, Oscar Lewis.

It may seem queer to today's young readers that an automobile would be considered something spectacular, but in 1893 it certainly was. The first car with a gasoline engine was made in Austria in the 1860's. (The steam-powered car came somewhat earlier.) Karl Benz, a German, made a one-cylinder gas-engine car in 1885 that could reach the speed of ten miles per hour.

Things were moving along in the United States, too. Research was being done on steam, electric, and gasoline-powered horseless carriages. We know the electric car was in use late in 1889 as a taxi in Chicago because a pedestrian was run down by one in that year.

The buggyaut was a real vehicle. In 1895, one with a two-cylinder gas engine and steered by a tiller raced over a grueling fifty miles at five miles per hour. (By 1902, a car could reach the speed of fifty-five miles per hour.)

Henry Ford produced his first automobile in 1893. It is fact that the other mechanical genius of the day, Thomas Alva Edison, advised Ford to stick with the gas engine because the batteries of the electric cars were too heavy and needed recharging while steam cars required a fire and a cumbersome boiler.

Auto making proceeded apace throughout the nineties, so we may presume that Elbert Bingham prospered. By 1900 there were 4,192 automobiles, though out of them only 936 were powered by gas engines. (Also, by this time the first auto show had come into being.)

I've mentioned other inventions of the late nineteenth century, such as the telephone. By 1902, there were over two million of them in the country. Electric lights were still an exciting novelty in 1893. One of the attractions of the Chicago Fair of that year was the electrically lit Electricity Building. Something else was being developed at that time, though it would not be unveiled until 1896, the first motion-picture show.

The pride and joy of my fictional volunteer firemen is a Silsby steam-powered fire engine. It was a real engine and a vast improvement over its hand-pumped predecessors.

In writing about mechanical innovations, it may seem out of context to discuss lace making. I've referred here to a special type of nineteenth-century lace called Carrickmacross. There was such a lace made only in Ireland and using the very motifs I have mentioned. (Readers will guess that the clover motif was really the traditional shamrock.) A special circular pattern done in crochet lace was also typical of Irish needlework and would have been recognizable to someone knowledgeable in such matters.

In researching this book I've become indebted to a number of people, among them Dr. Robert L. Friend and Dr. Robert Epstein, both dentists, and chemistry professor Dr. Harry Johnson, of the University of California, Riverside. Professor Johnson, who takes a special interest in the history of science, has helped me with previous books I have written as well. I am much indebted to Bay Area residents Marion R. Roth and Professor Eugene R. Purpus, who very graciously provided me with hard-to-find facts about San Francisco. They found what now-demolished buildings looked like before the disastrous 1906 earthquake and fire and where they were actually located. I must also thank Sharon Cline of the University of California, Riverside, Library for her reference work in my behalf.

Patricia Beatty
June, 1978

## About the Author

Now a resident of Southern California, Patricia Beatty was born in Portland, Oregon. She was graduated from Reed College there, and then taught high-school English and history for four years. Later she held various positions as science and technical librarian and also as a children's librarian. Quite recently she has taught Writing Fiction for Children in the Extension Department of the University of California, Los Angeles. She has had a number of historical novels published by Morrow, several of them dealing with the American West in the 1860 and 1895 period.

With her late husband, Dr. John Beatty, Mrs. Beatty also coauthored a number of books. One of them, *The Royal Dirk*, was chosen as an Award Book by the Southern California Council on Children's and Young People's Literature. Subsequently Mrs. Beatty received another award from the Council for her Distinguished Body of Work.

Mrs. Beatty is now married to a professor of economics at the University of California, Riverside, and she has a married daughter, Alexandra Beatty Stewart.